The
Index
of Dreams

Vicky Matthews

Vicky Matthews was born in 1966 and grew up
in Somerset. She studied English Literature at
Edinburgh University and works as
a freelance writer and editor.
The Index of Dreams is her first novel.

Table of Contents

The Index of Dreams

This morning I woke up with a warm, fuzzy feeling, as though I was five years old again, waking in the small, south-facing bedroom of my childhood, the sun streaming in through casement windows and the view of Bathwick Meadows in the distance. The memory made me feel safe, as though everything in my world was just as it should be. My body was suffused with a feeling of peace and I realised that the most wonderful feeling of being alive isn't necessarily a zany, active thing, but you could feel the ecstasy within, coursing through your blood, even as you lay still.

I remember now. Last night I dreamt I went to The Index and I know that's what's given me this peaceful feeling. It makes me realise that lately – well, nearly always, for at least the last twenty years – I've been trying too hard to keep things going; to get up in the morning; to earn a living; keeping going because my body keeps going. That's why I've always wanted to go to The Index of Dreams, if it existed in real life. I don't want to jump from a multi-storey car-park or hang myself. I guess the nearest to The Index scenario would be to take a heroin overdose. But, the thing is, I don't know any drug dealers – not that kind of drug dealer, anyway. Also, someone once told me, the first time you take heroin you might just puke it up. And I don't want to have to keep taking it a few times before I can keep an overdose 'down', like I've become a druggie. I don't want to be found with a needle in my arm. I want something more dignified. Something beautiful. Something like The Index of Dreams.

1

The Temp

Surfacing from the deep slumber, it takes me a moment to realise where I am: marooned in my one-bedroom flat in Lewisham, the very same place I've been living for the last fifteen years. On blustery days, the sash windows rattle in their frames. All I can see is the blue of the sky and the occasional, racing cloud, making me feel like I'm in a small, white cabin on a ship, bobbing along, adrift.

I'd like to just lie here, enjoying the warm fuzzy feeling from my dream. But if I don't force myself up, I'll just stay here, thinking I should have gone in. I head to the shower and hose myself down like an animal ready for the slaughter. I don't know why that image comes to mind every time I'm in the power shower, but at some level it's part of the day's conveyor-belt process, a production line that leads slowly and inexorably towards death. A very slow death, to be sure, one that involves people in suits carrying out tiny movements on the computer keyboard each day. The superior robots look smug and come back from their temporary reprieve, their foreign holidays, looking even more smug. The way their lips curl imperceptibly upwards, like they've got it all sorted, like they've cracked the meaning of life, makes me want to puke, basically.

Even though I rarely see any of the clients, I need to look smart, and after my shower I put on a white shirt and a classic dark blue suit. I look like I'm going to a funeral. How appropriate.

I walk to the far end of the platform so I don't have to stand cheek-by-jowl with the suited-and-booted who exude wafts of perfume, hair-spray and aftershave as an indication that they're office-ready, prepared for the day at close quarters with commuters and clients alike. I'm feeling a little more sensitive than normal. Even from where I stand, at a distance, the merest whiff of paraben-laden body-spray is making me feel queasy.

The train cruises into the station, gliding like a bull-nose shark, and comes to a smooth halt. The commuters surge forward to the open doors. Frantic, willing mortals are suctioned into the body of the carriages, and the doors clamp shut behind us. The people pushing ahead of me have taken the few remaining seats, so I claim some standing space near the door. Packed tightly by the crush of bodies, I'm forced next to the graffiti-covered plastic bin; its see-through bag displays a takeaway coffee cup and a crushed Diet Coke can and I wonder if someone has been drinking Diet Coke for breakfast.

Replete, the shark-train sets off. Somewhere deep inside my intestines, I feel a coil of despair. Outside the station, the train grinds to a halt, waiting for a signal change. I look up from the bin, my eyes now level with the top buttons of a man's expensive-looking black over-coat and his blue-striped linen scarf, which is tied in a Parisian knot. A more natural, earthy aftershave emanates from him – notes of sandalwood, bergamot and something that reminds me of walking on the Mediterranean coast, perhaps wild sage or tarragon – in contrast to the toxic wafts coming from the other commuters. I stay facing his trendy, Parisian knot, protected by the aura.

He's talking to someone on his mobile, "...whether she's cancelled her subscription or not, I've absolutely no idea. It's none of my business any more. Yes," he says angrily. "Yes, everything gets forwarded." I'm quite surprised. He doesn't seem like the kind of person who'd raise his voice on the packed, yet subdued, morning train. I feel like saying to him, "It's okay to be stressed. Actually, it's quite reassuring to know I'm not the only stressed person round here." If I could tell him, I would.

The train jolts as it sets off again, and I'm thrown next to a woman's bouffant-styled hair. I can definitely smell hairspray and I begin to feel dizzy. I reach for a nearby bobble grip and, my arm stretched to the max, I hold on tight. Now the woman with the bouffant hair is between me and the posh, stripy-scarf guy.

I spot a free seat further up the carriage between a portly man and a woman in a pink trouser-suit. Someone has put their laptop case on the spare seat but I squeeze myself through the throng of bodies: "Excuse me...

excuse me… sorry… I'm just trying… thanks…" The portly man glances up at me and then at what's left of the 'middle seat' between him and the trouser-suited woman. He swivels his chunky thighs towards the aisle and I edge past. "Oops, sorry… thanks."

The trouser-suited woman stares resolutely at *Money Week*, her power-red mouth pursed, then snatches up the case and puts it on her lap. I wedge myself into the narrow slot of blue upholstered seat. I could take my copy of *Jane Eyre* out of my bag and read it, but there isn't much space to move my arms so I start reading the headlines on the newspaper that someone in the seat opposite is holding:

Gove is nuts. Boris is after my job.

Mother sells cannabis to send son to private school.

'Generation Rent' tires of London landlords.

How can you sell jeans for £5.99? Easy… pay people 23p an hour to make them.

The woman in the facing window seat has a toddler on her lap. Every now and then the toddler's face creases and just as a plaintive cry rises up, the woman jiggles him and points animatedly out the window.

"Look… look! What's that? See the train! What's that? Can you see the big digger, Max?"

I look to where the woman points: *Site acquired for future development*, and, beyond the sign, a bulldozer, cranes, tunnels, Portacabins, warehouses, housing estates, high rise blocks. As the train inches along the view changes in slow motion: a car park, the towering 'M' in the sky of a McDonald's, CCTV cameras, a sign: *Passengers must not pass beyond this point*, children in a playground, conservatories, traffic jams, workmen on the lines, people's back gardens, a burnt-out church, a graveyard – bodies laid neatly in parallel lines.

The train draws to another standstill. A sense of impatience in the carriage. The portly man's mobile erupts with a ring-tone that imitates an old-fashioned phone. Momentarily, I recall the grey rotary-dial telephone on my granny's polished hall table. Midsummer sunshine. Orange dahlias in a blue and white vase.

The man pulls the handset out of his pocket and flicks it open. "Hello... Stewart somebody? No... but it'll probably... no, but it'll... yes... yes... ah yes... I did hear a message at 7... I was in the middle of the... yes... well these people can't get... Well, they can't always get me all of the time... they'll just have to survive... Bye."

A man on the other side of the aisle is reading *Internal Auditing and Business Risk: Identity Theft – know the signs*. He rubs his eyes and runs his hands across his scalp, perspiring. The woman next to him, iPhone buds plugged into her ears, glances sideways and starts reading the book as well.

Strobes of sunlight travel across the near-stationary carriage and then, in a momentary burst of optimism, the train gathers pace, releasing tension within the confined, airless space. Windows that don't open hold the acrid perfumed-toilets' smell in our midst.

Cannon Street. A couple of the passengers with their heads thrown back, mouths agape, come to with a start, reaching in their pockets, checking for tickets, gathering their briefcases. The man in the seat opposite folds his newspaper. He holds it aloft while he opens his man-bag and, just for a split second, I glimpse a headline: *The Index of Dreams – 20-Year Ban to be Lifted*?

Neurons fire off in my body, reawakening dormant cells. Something starts to pulse, a pinprick of a beat, a rhythm that reminds me I'm alive. I stand up with the throng and move into the aisle. Splayed newssheet underfoot, already discarded, trodden. I want to stop and examine the papers, to try and find the article, but I'm obliged to keep pace with the human flow. I take myself out of the onward propulsion by sitting back down in one of the seats and wait for the multitude to pass. I pick up a muddy-foot-printed copy of *Metro* and scan through its pages within seconds. No mention of *The Index of Dreams*. Perhaps I imagined it? I walk along the deserted aisle and find a copy of *The Telegraph*. It was a broadsheet the man was holding. I speed-scan through *The Telegraph*, but still can't see anything. Perhaps it was in the Culture Section? A man in a fluorescent vest is moving through the carriage now, picking up the papers and food wrappings and putting them into a clear plastic sack.

Out on the station concourse, I pause momentarily. "This isn't the real me," I tell myself, "I'm just playing a role. Getting paid £21 an hour to play a role." I think about the people who get paid 23p an hour to make the discount supermarket 'jeggings' and remind myself how lucky I am.

I think about scouring the newspapers in W H

Smith, or buying all the broadsheets, to look again for the article. I check my watch. I'm going to be late, and my breathing feels rapid so I focus on moving forwards, onwards, across the concourse, down the stairs. On the platform opposite is a poster with images of a beach – not an English seaside, but 'a slice of bling' the poster says… maybe somewhere like Dubai, but I don't have time to read it as the underground train pulls in, obscuring the immaculate crescent of sand and the couple with their arms wrapped round each other.

Liverpool Street. Worley & Beresford Solicitors. I stand in the lobby and sign in. Sabina Upsell. Security-pass on a blue ribbon. I hope they don't want me to actually wear it around my neck. I take the lift up to the fourth floor and head to reception. The receptionist has a calm demeanour and moves with composure as she signs for a couriered parcel. I wonder if it would be easy to work somewhere like this all the time if I copied her, with her pressed white blouse, her subtle make-up and hint of a holiday tan. And the wedding ring. That might be a bit harder.

"Sabina Upsell? Ah, okay, I'll just let them know you're here…" She lifts the telephone handset. "Hi Tabitha, just to let you know the temp's here. The temp who's here for the two-day booking? To cover for Simon? Sorry…" A hint of a smile plays at her lips. "Yeah. I shouldn't call her 'the temp'… Sabina's here. Sabina Upsell." The receptionist replaces the handset. "The office manager will be with you in just a moment. Take a seat. Can I get you something to drink?"

"Oh, I'm fine, thanks."

I sit down on a low, leatherette couch and wait for Tabitha. On the coffee table in front of me is a carefully placed fan of magazines: *Money Week, The Lawyer, Tatler.* A classically handsome man in a sharp suit breezes up to the reception desk.

"Any calls from Binxit Faddons – can you tell them I'm in a meeting till 10? I don't want any calls going through to the temp. Thanks!" As he says "Thanks!" he taps the reception top with a baton of rolled paper.

A short, 'en bon point' woman squeezed into a grey trouser-suit approaches, leans across the desk towards the receptionist, and says in a lowered voice, "He's in a funny mood! He hates it when she's away! The thing is, he'll just have to lump it. We can't all be here 24/7. Some of us have got *a life*! He had me here till 7pm last night sorting through his filing tray. He needs *babying*. The best thing is to play along!"

The receptionist gives the grey-suited woman a 'knowing smile'. "Ssh… You don't want to put the temp off before she's even started!"

"He doesn't even know about…" The 'en bon point' woman pats her stomach. "He won't be best pleased. That'll be *three* away…" Then she purses her wrinkled, mirthful lips and convulses slightly, pretending to suppress a burst of laughter.

The receptionist gives the grey-suited woman 'a look' and casts her eyes towards me.

"Okay, no worries, I'll catch you later." She turns in my direction and I stand up. "Sabina? Tabitha." She extends a freckled hand with stubby fingers. "Sorry to keep you waiting there. Have you been offered a drink of anything yet?"

"I'm fine, thanks."

"No worries. So let's get going! I'll take you over to your desk."

Tabitha leads me over to a partitioned area, which houses two unoccupied workstations.

"Here we go. Sit yourself down."

I sit down on a swivel chair with bright blue fabric. It's quite low so I use the lever at the side to pump myself up to an ergonomic height. Tabitha plumps herself into the adjacent roller chair and paddles with her feet to wheel herself across.

"Great. Here we go." She taps a varnished nail on a yellow post-it note: "Temp03. P/word: green."

"Just log yourself on with these. You've used Case Management before? Super. We use LegalPrima at Worley & Beresford. Have you used LegalPrima before? …O…kay… Just have a poke around the desktop while I get you some of Simon's files. Get yourself comfortable. A bit of health and safety and all that."

As soon as Tabitha has disappeared, I click Google open and type *The Index of Dreams*. It's there. The article. Numerous articles.

The Index of Dreams – Ban to Be Lifted After 20 Years?

A New Era – Index of Dreams to be Uncensored

Is Ossian Brohmer Set to Re-emerge From his 20-Year Hibernation?

I click on the one about emerging from hibernation.

Georgette Coles speaks to the Swedish film director about the suppression of his award-winning film.

Where has the legendary film-maker been hiding for two decades? Tucked away in a frozen landscape somewhere, surviving on gravadlax and smoked reindeer?

Ossian Brohmer, now 55 years old and still decidedly striking, runs a hand through his pewter hair, and ignores my opening question. Instead, he offers me an espresso (made with freshly-ground beans) at his ramshackle, but charming, cliff-top home…

"We don't normally use the Internet for personal purposes, outside of the lunch-hour." I jump and spin round. Tabitha is standing behind me, holding a wad of grey files.

"Oh. Sorry about that." I click it shut.

Tabitha plumps herself back down into her chair. "Ooof! That's better! You'd be surprised with this job… how much you're actually on your feet all day. Ooof! O…kay… so… first we go into Commercial Property… like so…" Expertly shifting the mouse in a series of rapid movements, Tabitha clicks away. "You're working for Simon Beresford, so… anything on this list that is Simon's… then off you go into templates… Okay?"

"Mm hm."

"So… Worley & Beresford letterhead. Next… into the address book…"

"I think I remember how to use it now."

"Great. Wonderful! I'll leave you to it then, Sabina. Just ring me on 102 if you get stuck. Okay! Super duper. I'll see you later."

Deep down inside, something doesn't feel quite right. For some reason, I'm beginning to feel wobbly; sick. The computer monitor begins to swim in front of my eyes. I refocus. Right. Section 106 letter. Bring up the address for the other solicitors, whoever the other solicitors are. I flick through the Section 106, Hammersmith file. Normally it's a breeze to force myself into being a robot, but somehow I feel trapped; interrupted; desperate for air.

2

Parisian Knot

Luckily, the second task is amending a long lease. Luckily, because I can go into more of a lull as I gradually work my way through the pages, rather than dart in and out of different files and documents. Well, I could go into a lull except that I have to decipher the red felt-tip squiggles with which the document has been marked up. I wonder if they do it deliberately – write so illegibly. Each undulating word looks exactly the same, like wavelets on a sea, except for the initial letter. 'P...' squiggle, '36 ...' squiggle. I type in 'Part 36 offer'. 'S...' squiggle of 'D ...' squiggle = 'Schedule of Dilapidations', I guess.

Once I've typed up the accompanying email (marked 'urgent') I decide to find Simon Beresford, so he can check the documents and then I can ping them off to the other side. He must be the smug guy who tapped his baton of paper on the reception desk – "I don't want any calls going through to the temp!"

I walk along the corridor and stand outside a door with the nameplate 'Simon Beresford', holding the draft documents. I'm about to knock, when I hear the sound of filing cabinet drawers being slammed shut, as though with an angry bang. A really angry bang. SLAM! SLAM! SLAM! I stand there anxiously, my hand poised to knock. I wait. I can't stand here all day, so I tap on the door.

"Yes?" says a male voice.

I edge the door open.

"Sorry... I just..."

A tall, quirky-looking man is standing at the window. His cheeks are flushed red and he looks ill-at-ease. It's not the smug, baton-of-paper-holding man I saw earlier. I catch an aroma of bergamot or cedarwood in this unlikely setting, this expanse of grey with a large formica desk and a floor-to-ceiling window that looks out onto a tower of glass and steel across the road, which also has floor-to-ceiling windows. Then I see his linen scarf splayed across the back of his chair and I realise it's the man from the train. The one with his scarf tied in a Parisian knot. The one who I wanted to stay standing next to, protected from the paraben-laden perfume of the other commuters.

"I just..."

"Do you need me to sign something?"

"If you could just check this urgent..."

"No problem."

I step forwards and wait at his desk while he speed-reads through the documents.

I look down at the doodles he's scrawled on the paperwork of the file that's open on his desk. Spirals in biro, pressed deep into the paper. Into file copies and even original letters from other solicitors. Star shapes and scribbled notes at messy angles. I've never seen that before. I wonder if he worries what the Solicitors Regulation Authority will think if they ever check his files.

"Excellent. Perfect." He proffers the documents back. "If you can get that scanned in and emailed across… Has Tabs shown you how to scan?"

"No… but… I can probably work it out."

I'm half way through the door when he asks: "Didn't I see you on the train this morning? You got on at Lewisham?"

I turn round. "Yes, that's right." Then I continue through the door.

3

An Interview with Ossian Brohmer

Is Ossian Brohmer Set to Re-emerge From his 20-Year Hibernation?

Georgette Coles speaks to the Swedish film director about the suppression of his award-winning film.

Where has the legendary film-maker been hiding for two decades? Tucked away in a frozen landscape somewhere, surviving on gravadlax and smoked reindeer?

Ossian Brohmer, now 55 years old and still decidedly striking, runs a hand through his pewter hair, and ignores my opening question. Instead, he offers me an espresso (made with freshly-ground beans) at his ramshackle, but charming, cliff-top home on the south coast.

I admit I had been expecting some evidence of his Swedish heritage within the house, but clearly Brohmer is a man whose mind has been on matters more pressing than refurbishment.

"I have fought certain demons… creative demons since The Index was banned."

I ask him whether this was compounded by his receiving a Razzie (Golden Raspberry) for Worst Picture in 1996 for his 'come-back' film The Blue Snowflake.

"Not that old chestnut again!" complains Brohmer, good-humouredly. "The thing is, right now, I'm in a good place, knowing that people will get to see The Index of Dreams. There's a whole generation out there who tell me they've been waiting to see it. The thing is, it clearly struck a chord. People need to be free to discuss their impulses, to see them represented in books and films, to be able to say how they really feel about things. I mean, look at mental health issues in today's society. It's not as though we're making a particularly good job of it, right? And at the end of the day, it's just a story. I didn't make the film to debate euthanasia. It's just a story, right? One that explores certain emotions… frees up… gives free reign to certain emotions…"

I sip the very good espresso that the award-winning film-maker has served me in a small, delicate cup, and concur. Word on the ground has it that no release date has actually been set. How does he feel about this?

"I don't know," responds Brohmer, with more than a little (perhaps justified) irritation. Why not ask the censor-ship board? It's only taken them twenty years to make up their minds."

Sensing I've touched his Achilles heel – after all, the once up-and-coming director was set to become Tinsel Town's golden boy before his long hibernation – I move onto fresher ground. Is it true that a new film is in the offing?

Brohmer squints and looks towards the seascape that glitters in the distance. "It's true there is a project… a script. I'm working with some students from The Met Film School… just a low budget, fun project, really… it's great to have these young people on board, all gaining experience on set. We've just started a mood board, to get a sense of the thing, before the story is completed."

Given that no-one has filled the gap left by Brohmer all these years, I'll definitely be keeping my ear to the ground on this one. Oh, and looking out for that release date for The Index of Dreams…

4

Slim Pickings

"It's lunch-time! You're not still working are you?" Tabitha approaches my partition, a sandwich in one hand. "There's a buffet in the conference room. A leaving party for one of the secretaries. She pats her stomach and smiles mirthfully. "It never rains but it pours! That's the second one off on maternity leave! Anyway, you're very welcome to participate. There's all sorts… sandwiches, including vegetarian, posh crisps, cherry tomatoes, fruit… oh, and cake, of course."

"Thank you."

Tabitha steps a little nearer and lowers her voice in a conspiratorial whisper. "I'm not supposed to say anything yet… I haven't cleared it with HR or anything, but just to let you know, we've got a couple of openings coming up for legal support."

"Oh, thank you. I wasn't quite sure, though, whether I wanted to be a secretary any more. I guess that's why I'm temping."

"We don't have secretaries here. We have *legal support*. A flat structure. No hierarchy. And these guys are *very generous*. I just thought I'd put a word in as you've managed to keep Simon happy all morning!"

"Oh, okay, thank you. It's just… I don't feel very well at the moment. I'm kind of thinking of taking a break."

Tabitha takes a bite of her sandwich and nods while she chews. "Okay… no worries. It's just a thought. Have a think. See how you get on. I'd better get back to the conference room. You might as well grab a free sandwich or two, even if you want to put it on a serviette and get back to your social media, online news or whatever… Ossian Brohmer? That's a funny name. Who's he when he's at home?"

Unofficially, it's obviously a 'do' for the women. For what-ever reason, the men have avoided the 'leaving' buffet. Apart from one. I'm surprised to see Simon Beresford sitting there, dutifully talking to one of the secretaries, looking awkward, a paper plate with a selection of buffet offerings balanced on his knees. I can't just put food on a plate and leave immediately. Perhaps I should have just headed to Pret a Manger. Slunk off. Independent. Done my own thing.

The far end of the conference table showcases the 'Sorry You're Leaving' cards and presents: a baby-grow, hand-knitted booties, a basket with organic baby toiletries, something shaped like a cake, wrapped in a white cloth.

There's a bowl of cherry tomatoes. They look like good ones. Genuinely ripe. I take a paper plate and balance a small handful of the tomatoes on top, add a spoon of hummus to the side and then eyeball the sandwiches to assess if there's anything edible. An avocado salad wrap? Despite the awkwardness, it's worth taking advantage, and I add it to the plate. I grab a can of Diet Coke from the drinks table and I'm heading for the door when Tabitha approaches and tugs at my arm.

"You made it! I know you probably want to get back to your social media, but have you seen the cake? You *must* see the cake!" Back at the table she shows me the towelling-encased cylinder that's tied with a cerise polka-dot ribbon. A small cloth rabbit sits on the top, holding a marzipan announcement: 'Yummy Mummy To Be'.

"Isn't it *a hoot*! You've got your Belgian chocolate slab inside your cotton nappy; and then the cuddly toy for the little one."

"Wow. It's really nice."

"It's a very *sociable* firm. We always take time out to celebrate the big events. Birthdays. Christmas. These are one bunch of generous guys that we work for. It's a full package, really, at Worley & Beresford."

"I have to say, the lunch looks nice! It's very *women*-friendly. Quite a lot of women."

"Oh, you'll find slim pickings here. The guys are all married… well, except…"

"I didn't come to Worley & Beresford to try and find a husband, I can *assure* you."

Back at my desk I scroll through images from *The Index of Dreams*. Stina and Albin. Stina running away to find The Index of Dreams. All I know is what Andrea Rosenhay told me all those years ago. I imagine I'm waiting at Gothenburg Station. Waiting at the appointed time to be taken to The Index, as though I'm Stina. But then I find myself thinking how, if I was seventeen again, I'd like to explore… to see if I could do things differently. Have a different outcome. Maybe I'd like to go for a walk in the forest first, or lots of walks in the forest. And then go back to the appointed place at Gothenburg Station another time. Save The Index itself for later, maybe.

I stare out the window and find myself recalling the aroma of Simon Beresford's aftershave. The slamming drawers. The doodles. And then I go over what Slim Pickings said about all the guys being married… From now on, I think I'll call her Slim Pickings.

"Sorry about that."
I jump and turn round. It's Simon.
"Oh, about what?"
"The excruciating lunch."
"Oh. I thought the food was okay."
He looks directly at me, and smiles slightly.

5

The Realm of Dreams

17:34. Cannon Street to Lewisham. I sit on the train, watching the scenery in reverse: the graveyard – bodies laid neatly in parallel lines, the burnt-out church, people's back gardens, traffic jams, conservatories, a sign *Passengers must not pass beyond this* point, CCTV cameras, the towering 'M' of a McDonald's, a car park… Pink cherry blossom floats on the breeze; spring sunshine lights the graffitied embankment. Blossom? Is summer nearly here? Perhaps I should go on a mini-break. *Do* something this weekend, like everybody else.

18:20. Back home, I flick open my lap-top.

In reality, the impact of Ossian Brohmer and *The Index* had gradually been receding from my world up until 2008, the year when I first got Broadband. Up until that point, it was a fading teenage obsession, if you like, that had been interspersed with other mini-obsessions and forays into connecting with real life that involved various short-term relationships and adventures.

Anyway, Ossian had been off the radar for so long that I was surprised by the multitude of photos and interviews/video clips – all available at the click of a button. This abundance caused neurons to fire off in my brain, reactivated the passion I'd once felt for Ossian's image and the music from *The Index of Dreams,* as well as its concept. And not only resuscitated it, but enabled it to evolve because, for the first time, I could hear Ossian talking, absorb his voice, see his mannerisms. And all this had a *life,* a *depth,* an *attraction,* that seemed missing in the outer world – in the flat desert of reality, of life as I knew it, as I'd been experiencing it in the intervening years. I knew other people would think I was mad. But I didn't care. If this was the only thing that triggered such feeling, then I was quite entitled to it, and nobody else need even know about it. It wasn't that I based my life around it, not my day-to-day existence of going through the motions; but whenever I dipped into the film music, the images, the video clips, it was as though a vibration reached me; held within it was a feeling I could connect with; a note, a tone that understood a pain at the core; allowed what was hidden to exist; something that said *this is real feeling.*

The photos taken on set of *The Index* gave me some insight into the film – into the forbidden mythical reality. Yes, I'd been denied the full story, the moving images, during the cinema debacle back in 1994, but there were some stills, at least, that I could examine in minute detail.

The character of Stina was played by a young actress called Albertina Karlsson, and I paid particularly close attention to the shots of her and Ossian on set together. In one of my favourites they're standing in the snow outside Gothenburg Central Station. Just in frame are the cameraman and the sound engineer with the boom and, centre stage, Albertina looks towards Ossian, who's totally focussed, his graceful hands cupped as though around an imagined ball of energy.

If it was possible to transport yourself to being anyone at any moment in time, I would have chosen to be Albertina on set with Ossian. Although, logically, she would perhaps have been too young to be in a relationship with Ossian (even though he was only in his early thirties at that point, Albertina would have been around sixteen), in my fuzzy daydream anything is possible – if only a feeling, an admiration, a worship that could be tapped into later, in years to come. Because if someone had asked me if there was anyone on the planet I would marry without hesitation, without meeting them beforehand even, it would be Ossian Brohmer.

My favourite YouTube clip was an interview with him in Paris. In the opening frame, he's leaning on a pillar next to an ornate wrought-iron gate that leads onto a paved, planted courtyard. The camera follows him inside a villa built in the style of turn-of-the-century Nouvelle Athens architecture. I remember him talking about using a special filter for *The Index of Dreams* – a golden-yellow filter that gave uniformity. Although it was a film about death, he used the golden filter to give it a warmth. He wanted the experience of the film to be like entering another world, a world of pure emotion.

After this discovery of images and interviews all at the click of a button, I was like a laboratory mouse that becomes addicted to a substance – a mouse that returns to the button and presses it over and over for a repeat experience. The problem was, that after that initial glut of information, very little new material became available over the years. And my favourite interview, the one on location in Paris, actually disappeared one day.

But, with today's new bounty of information, there's a photo of Ossian that I haven't seen before. Alongside the article about emerging from hibernation, he's featured standing on a beach that's more reminiscent of the English seaside than a desolate Swedish coastline. A beach that looks strangely familiar, that makes me wonder if I've absorbed something of the Nordic environment without being aware of it – gleaned from a book, a film... or visited it in the realm of dreams, perhaps.

6

The Point of Collapse

The next morning I take my usual place on the platform, at the far end, away from the wafts of paraben-laden commuters and when the train slithers into view, in the distance, I feel a pinprick of awkwardness in my solar plexus. The steel snake draws nearer and I'm aware that carried in one of its segments, possibly, is Simon Beresford. Should my strategy be to stand in the same place so that I get into the same carriage as before? Does *he* get into the same carriage every day? But if I get into the same carriage and he's there, will he think that I've *deliberately* got into the same carriage? I walk a few steps further back into the throng in order to keep life simple.

The doors of the snake bounce open to reveal the congestion within. Bodies full to the brim in this particular compartment, teetering on the edge, in danger of spilling out. I rush along to the next carriage and insert myself in a small gap between bodies before the doors clamp shut. There's no aroma of bergamot or cedarwood.

But that's okay. A relief. Because I'm not looking to meet anyone. Not within the confines of a solicitors' office. I stare down at the grey plastic bin-top. Don't look down, look up. That's what someone once told me. I look at the complexion of the woman I'm sandwiched against. Thick foundation. Red lipstick. Fortified. Perhaps in it for the long-term. I glance around and see a yellow tie with blue space invaders, a pink tie with flashes of colour, a black tie with orange and gold. Dark grey clothes, navy clothes, black clothes, in contrast to the celebrity in the paper that the foundation-clad woman is holding: *Chloe goes from beach babe to boho chic as she rocks two outfits in one day.* Beneath the headline is a photo of a tanned girl in a colourful cutaway swimsuit. *Cheeky! Chloe showcases a pert posterior in her daring, self-designed one-piece.*

I'm near enough to a bobble-grip to hold on. To keep me upright until journey's end. At London Bridge the train expels half of its contents. A few more bodies embark. I install myself in one of the free seats. I stare out the window and think back to Slim Pickings with her mirthful, wrinkled smile, a stash of rings on her wedding finger and her mouse-mat that features three of her grandchildren, Reuben, Rocco and Harper. Even though she's quite *en bon point* and boring as hell, she managed to seal the deal and reproduce; and then her offspring, too, produced sproglets. Six in total so far, "…and counting."

I make it to the downstairs foyer of the block that houses Worley & Beresford when I begin to feel slightly dizzy. In the mirrored lift, I assess my reflection. In my imagination, I look like a city slicker, but I see a lost child looking back at me, a West Country hippie in my mum's old tweed jacket, full of uncertainty.

The lift doors ping open onto the fourth floor landing.

I say "Hi!" to the receptionist and make my way along the corridor, back to my desk. Well, actually it's not *my* desk, it's the desk of someone called Melinda Chlebek, who I'm covering for. Is she Polish? Or maybe Lithuanian? I marvel that someone can transplant themselves into a new life in a new country, learn a new language and get it all sorted. Marriage, baby, career – although… maybe this isn't *a career*, exactly. She's already got two children, judging by the photos of smiling, cherubic offspring: a school photo; another one shows them *en famille* playing on the beach, together with the hands-on dad.

I switch on the computer and click on LegalPrima and the task-list. Someone's already left the files I'll need – two towers of grey folders – on the floor by my desk. There's a 10-minute letter to type. Fowler & Smallwood, 36 Hermitage Road. I clamp the headphones on.

"Sabina, on the Fowler file, could you please type a letter to Art Hansford…"

Simon Beresford's voice activates some sub-atomic energy particles within my cells. I wonder if it's a survival mechanism, to project romantically onto someone in this environment, in order to create motivation.

"Good morning, Sabina! Have you got yourself a coffee or something?" Tabitha's standing next to the pile of files, nursing a pink mug decorated with cartoonish flowers and the statement, 'Glamorous Granny!'

"Oh, don't worry – I'm fine, thanks."

"Just to let you know, once you've run out of work, we'll transfer you over to Corporate. They've got a bit of a backlog!"

"What about Simon?"

"Simon? He's away now. Away for the bank holiday weekend. Picking up his kids from Northampton. His youngest kids, that is. He's got two older ones in America as well – but that's another story. I've got six arriving tomorrow myself! Doing anything special yourself? Got any plans?"

"To be honest, I didn't realise it *was* bank holiday..."

"So, just give me a buzz when you're freed up."

Tabitha's figure recedes down the corridor and then I'm alone again. Suddenly, I can't stand the sight of all the office paraphernalia. The yellow post-it notes. The mug with some company logo on it. The ball of elastic bands. The special office-tidy with which Melinda Chlebek has customised her desk, which dispenses one paper clip at a time through some magnetic mechanism. The set of drawers beneath the desk, full of her cup-a-soups, mints and her can of spray-on deodorant. I force myself to keep going. It's only a two-day booking after all. Temping. A short sprint, so you're always approaching the finish line. Always approaching a mini-reprieve.

11am. I look for a file amongst the teetering pile of grey manila folders. Not there. I head to Simon's office. Despite the fact he's not here today, I knock, just in case, and gingerly open the door. Empty. I go in and although I'm doing what I'm supposed to be doing – looking for a file in his filing cabinet – I take the opportunity to glance around. A couple of Tae Kwon-do trophies sit on top of a bookcase. A photo of Simon in his white Tae Kwon-do outfit – black belt – at an awards ceremony. A school photo of two girls aged around six and seven. I find the file and quickly exit.

11.30am. Six hours to go to reach the next milestone in my life, the safety of sitting alone in my flat, wondering if there is any direction I can take that will ever *change* anything.

"*…loss or damage by fire and such other risks as the Landlord considers prudent to insure against on the basis that such insurance is available in the market on reasonable terms acceptable to the Landlord… We look forward to hearing from you with the amendments at your earliest convenience. Yours faithfully… etcetera.*"

Although there *is* one thing that has changed. *Or talk* that something may change. The supposed release of *The Index of Dreams.* But, at the end of the day, it's only a film; it isn't *real.* It doesn't mean I can actually check in at The Index of Dreams.

It might be okay if I could just sit here, typing, listening to the familiarity of Simon Beresford's voice. But the transfer to Corporate, the energy required to absorb anything new whatsoever…

Save. File. Print.

I feel the slight nausea again and wonder if I'm going to make it through to 5.30pm. I head to the loo and look in the mirror. My face is completely white. Perhaps I am actually ill.

✷

"You're not supposed to be here! What are *you* doing here?" It's Slim Pickings a little further down the corridor. Her voice purrs, "But it's your day off! Nothing can be *that urgent* on your day off! We all need our *down time!*"

Then I hear the murmur of a male voice. A voice that triggers an explosion, the creation of a new mini-universe, galaxies shooting off in all directions, in my solar plexus – even though I feel ill, and even though I had no idea that Simon Beresford actually existed 28 hours ago.

"…some urgent emails to check… just en route… thought I'd swing by… traffic not too bad, considering…"

I walk to the printer and collect the letter. Strategy. Just keep acting normally. Find lease in the file. Run it through the photocopier, to scan it. Focussed. Casual. Natural. I manage to get back to the workstation and that's when I feel my legs giving way. I crumple and have the sensation of a blissful black tunnel rushing to meet me.

I absorb the healing smell of the cologne. Cypress? Juniper berry? A hint of bergamot transports me somewhere sunny, rugged, Mediterranean. Sun on bare skin. Dry heat. Aromatic herbs. I can hear Simon's voice, sounding far away. Or not far away, but as though I'm in a different sphere, at one remove from everything.

I feel someone putting something soft underneath my head.
Slim Pickings: "Should we call an ambulance?"

Simon: "I'll just try the recovery position for a minute."

I feel agile hands carefully manoeuvring me onto my side, gently bending one knee and one arm. And I think how much nicer it feels than when a man normally touches me… how right it feels, compared to all the touching with sexual intent, touching with an end-goal in mind. Fingertips exert a gentle pressure on my wrist pulse.

Simon: "She's breathing okay, but maybe we *should* call a paramedic."

Slim Pickings: *"Shall* I call a paramedic?"

Simon: "She looks very pale. Sabina? Can you hear me, Sabina?"

I open my eyes and make the effort to speak, "…be fine in a few minutes… perhaps I'll go home… be fine."

"You'll need to stay lying down for a while. Maybe get a glass of water, Tabs." Simon's crouched beside me. Wearing 'off duty' gear. Sporty clothes, as if he could be en route to a game of squash or off for a run. Despite the illness, it feels like a special moment. A moment that gives you permission to feel like a character in a Regency novel. Permission to be weak. Permission to feel rescued. Mills & Boon.

Slim Pickings brings a glass of water and I sit up and take a few sips before lying down again. She seems genuinely concerned and I decide that maybe I should think of her as Tabitha again, after all.

When the taxi arrives, Simon accompanies me downstairs to the foyer, carrying my bag. "Don't worry about the timesheet. I'll make sure it's signed off for the whole day. I'll put the taxi on expenses… Get plenty of rest. Doing anything special for the Bank Holiday?"

I shake my head. It's probably just the illness, but I feel a lump in my throat. A temptation to let tears out.

Out through the swing doors. The sun seems too bright. I'm not quite well yet. I definitely need to lie down in a dark room.

He opens the cab door for me and it's too bad that I'll probably never see him again.

He's handing me his card, though.

"I don't know how I'd have managed without you these last couple of days. If you ever need a reference..."

And then he closes the door and the taxi pulls away.

7

Vanilla Sex

"Of course you can come and convalesce at mine, Beanie. You should partake of the sea air, it will do you a world of good."

"You sound like some maiden aunt in a Victorian novel."

"Well, I hope I don't look like one."

I picture Louis in his Breton jumper, his dark hair slicked back over a trendy undercut, and, despite his forty-five years, the sprung look that evidences his regular efforts at toning and body sculpting.

"Not *too* much."

"I mean, I like cross-dressing and everything… but maybe something a bit more up-to-date?"

The signal breaks up and his voice begins to wobble, punctuated by blips of silence, like some kind of Morse code.

"Louis?... Louis?"

"There's–––––storm brewing––––windy–––so I was

going to————just when——don't you think?———typical———
Bank Holiday..."

I hear the sound of a door bang shut and imagine
Louis standing on his Art Deco, sea-view balcony, his
slicked hair lifted up by the wind.

"Hang on... I'm just going in. That's better."

"So, you're sure it's okay to stay for a few days?"

"Absolument. And there's so much to do here.
Apparently it's now Notting-Hill-on-Sea, according
to the Sunday supplements. There's this amazing new
bar called The Candy Box and it's full to bursting with
really interesting women who keep telling me I'm their
gay best friend. By the way, I know some women who
would really appreciate you, Sabina."

"Not that old chestnut. Anyway, this guy where I
was temping... he was quite nice."

"Saucy! So... did you tell him?"

"Tell him what?"

"That you fancy him!"

"Of course not! I've finished temping there, anyway.
All I'm saying is that when I was listening to his voice,
it had an effect on me. A reaction at a cellular level."

"You can look his number up on the website,
can't you?"

"I'm not going to ring him. No way! Don't be ridiculous. I only told you about the effect his voice had on me
because I was trying to explain..."

"But how can you hope to... *you know*... if you don't
even speak to him?"

"I'm not hoping to...!"

"Well, what are you hoping for then?"

"Very funny."

"Or, maybe you're worried… about… you know..."

"What?"

"Your little problem… in the bedroom."

"Oh, you mean being dysfunctional?" Normally I only like certain things, like being massaged, or being stroked very delicately, preferably with my clothes on. "I only like vanilla sex, it's true."

"Vanilla sex? You mean like the missionary position?"

"No... I thought vanilla sex meant just stroking and things?"

"Are you *serious?*"

"So what kind of sex is just stroking and things?"

"That's called *not having sex*. I don't think I'll be introducing you to the dark rooms just yet…"

"The *dark* rooms?"

"Anyway, some of the chic lesbians at The Candy Box, they just pretend, they put their arms around each other and kiss a bit and probably not much more. And, like I said, I know some women – *chic* women – who would really appreciate you, Sabina."

8

Le Petit Mort

I wake up and watch clouds racing across the skylight. A fierce sea wind shoos away the grey, revealing patches of blue. Now just small cumuli sail by, as white and unthreatening as balls of cotton wall.

Finally, I get up and walk around the well-appointed apartment, which, in Louis's estate agency speak, would be described as, "Art Deco With a Sea View. Generous proportions and high ceilings add immense appeal to this two-bedroom property, with original features throughout the building, from the parquet flooring to the stone stair-case with original chrome balustrade." I stand on the balcony, my hands resting on the wrought-iron top rail, looking out at grey waves gilded with light, thinking that perhaps Quinton-on-Sea has a certain appeal, after all. Even the storm within, the nausea, has passed; a poison lifted and dispelled, like a cloud.

I peek round Louis' bedroom door. There's the sound of a light, steady snore and a motionless form beneath an ocean of down duvet. Tiptoeing away, I head to the kitchen, help myself to a glass of orange juice from Louis' fancy, retro fridge, then venture out in search of a double espresso in one of the seafront cafes. Hot sun breaks through the remaining cloud suddenly and unexpectedly. The shore is entirely deserted. I take the steps down to the beach and stretch out on the warmed pebbles, near the Pier, and start humming *Under The Boardwalk*. Seagulls whirl and cry above the surf. In the distance I can see the mini-funfair: a big plastic apple with a roller-coaster that, in holiday season, tunnels through it like a maggot, the 'speed wave' carousel and the merry-go-round. It's all at a standstill, but I imagine I can smell the vanilla of the Mr Whippy ice-cream, and suddenly I long for a soft, twirled ice-cream. It's too exquisite, though – this feeling of lying in the sun. Too heavy to stir, I just want to lie, semi-comatose, with the hot sun on my face and my neglected body, pulsing life back into me.

The pebbles are so warm from the sun. I close my eyes and listen to the waves crashing against the shingle and the wave-breakers.

Despite the fact that I'm not at work right now, so I don't need the 'projecting-romantic-longings-onto-someone' survival mechanism, strangely I find myself thinking about Simon Beresford. The smell of his cologne. The flicker of a conspiratorial smile. Private. A message. His hands moving me into the recovery position. A door into another world. My thoughts become hazy and I think back to the 'dark rooms' that Louis mentioned. What did he mean? I imagine myself lying

in a dark room on a bed, naked apart from my underwear – underwear that's a bit more risqué than my usual
preference – and Simon Beresford comes in. I'm not quite
sure, in my reverie, whether I'm supposed to know it's
him in the dark, or even whether he knows it's me there.

Usually, my fantasies never get past second base, or
even first base – someone holding my hand or someone
stroking my hair – but suddenly I'm able to imagine
everything, feel exactly what happens in the dark room.
I hear myself cry out, a series of strange, soft animal
cries. I realise I've always tried too hard before to make
myself feel something when I didn't feel anything at all.
I didn't realise that it was something that would happen
to me. There's something pleasingly impersonal about it,
beautifully objective, untouched by all the debris, the
neurosis, of my previous attempts with the opposite sex.

I'm quite still, lying next to the wave-breaker, the
sound of me mixing with the sound of the surf.

9

The Forbidden Apple

"I've only just got up and now it's raining again!" Louis emerges from his bedroom, rubbing his eyes. "Was it busy out there? It's totally buzzy these days, don't you think? I know you think it's a bit down-at-heel, and maybe it is compared to *Bath,* Beanie, but the thing is… the thing is… where would you rather be living? Here? Or Lewisham?"

"Mm, I know what you're saying. It was quite nice lying on the beach just now. But if I moved from Lewisham, I could move *anywhere.* Well, not quite *anywhere,* but lots of places!"

"But the sea air… you already look a zillion times better!"

"Do I?"

"Yeah, like totally relaxed and chilled out. Cappuccino?"

"Mm, okay!"

I run my index finger along the shelves that house Louis's DVD collection. "How about we watch a film after lunch? Since it's raining…" My finger comes to rest on *The Double Life of Veronique.*

"We've watched that before, Beanie!"

"I know."

"How many times?"

"Maybe four? Five? I'd really love to watch it again."

"It's symptomatic, Beanie – that you don't let enough new things into your life. It's like your wardrobe situation. You really could venture beyond wearing just jeans and T-shirts."

"But I've saved so much money as a result of not being conned by the fashion industry! You know, I invested it – into bricks and mortar."

"Ah, yes, the palatial abode in Lewisham…"

"…and like the holidays I didn't take, the car I didn't drive, the restaurant meals I didn't eat – all invested into bricks and mortar. I thought you might appreciate that, being an estate agent."

"Yes, but a home is just the starting point from which to go out and have fun, not somewhere to bury yourself away all the time… Anyway, at least watch a film that you haven't seen before. Look, *Unrelated?* The box set of *This is England?*"

We watch *The Double Life of Veronique*, then *Unrelated.* Followed by two episodes of *This is England*, and I decide I quite like being a convalescent.

Later, I'm reading the titles on the spines of the DVD collection again – two whole rows that neatly span

Louis's bookshelves – when I notice something that jolts me. I slide the DVD from its place on the shelf and hold it in my hands.

"I can't believe it! How did you get hold of this?"

"Get what? Oh, *that!* It's a bit teen-angsty for my taste, these days."

"But how come you've got a copy? How?"

"Oh… mmm… oh, that's right, I bought it at the local arts cinema…"

I stare at the cover, reeling with shockwaves that I've actually got it in my hands. The cover image is a black and white close-up of Albertina as Stina. Although she's a teenager, she has an uncertain, child-like expression.

The Index of Dreams
You weren't born to struggle and you don't have to struggle any more

I flip the DVD case over and read the blurb:

Set at an unspecified date in the future, The Index of Dreams chronicles the lives of two teenagers drawn to one another through their shared experiences of childhood trauma. Unwilling to live with the consequences, or the struggle to overcome it, they travel to The Index of Dreams, an institute where controversial scientist, Dr Nordholm, has set up a radical experiment. At the institute, suicidal people are free to socialise, share their thoughts about death without the pressure to be 'cured' by optimism, and even, if they so choose, to never wake up ever again. Will anyone return from the Index of Dreams?

- Swedish, with English subtitles.

Below the blurb is a sound bite from a review:

The pyjama party where you never have to wake up.

I turn the DVD in my hands, absorbing the cover once more. *The Index of Dreams.* The forbidden apple. Then I flip to the back again. There's an inset with a small black and white photo of Ossian Brohmer.

Ossian Brohmer was born in Gothenburg and attended the New York Film Academy. He is a highly-acclaimed, award-winning film-maker. His 1994 film The Index of Dreams premiered at Cannes and won Best Feature at The Berlin International Film Festival later that year.

The small black-and-white photo is a recent one. He looks directly towards the camera with a diffident expression, the expression of someone who knows who they are, someone who doesn't have to try too hard. I think of all the photos of me with scrunched-up, awkward expressions, photos that I threw away, or begged people to delete from their phones, and wonder what it's like to be naturally elegant, to have a whole series of portraits to show to the world – to show the world who you really are.

"Don't you think this photo of Ossian Brohmer proves that you can have completely grey hair and still be completely good looking? I think he looks even better *now* than when he was younger!"

"I guess so…"

"Anyway, how come they were selling it at The Little Picture House? I thought it was still censored."

"I don't know, darling. They showed it at The Moving Images festival back in March, and Ossian was there…"

"Stop… Stop… Wait… He was there in *real life*?"

"Ye…es…"

"In *real life*?"

"Ye…es…"

"So, wait… Hang on… What was he doing here? *Here*! In *Quinton-on-Sea*?"

"Well, you know, since they were showing the film… he was giving one of those artsy-fartsy introductions… got all the suckers to buy his DVDs, too… promotional copies or something; except he was selling them. Thought it might be worth getting a copy since it's still banned. Probably worth a mint on eBay…"

"Did you actually *speak* to him?"

"I think I shook hands with him on the way out… maybe said something like, 'Cheers, mate!'"

"'Cheers, mate!' To *Ossian Brohmer*? 'Cheers, mate?' And you've seen the film… I feel kind of sick that I missed it. That I missed seeing *him*."

"I thought I mentioned it to you at the time – well, maybe not Ossian, but the festival – anyway… I don't know… sometimes you're not very definite about actually doing things."

I sit down on the sofa and bury my head in my hands.

"Hey! If I'd known it was such a big deal to you, Beanie, I'd have told you! I'd have rung you up and said 'Hey, Ossian Brohmer, who once made a film 20 years ago, is giving this talk!' But you know, if you're interested in people who were once in a pop band or once had a book published or have a zillion art exhibitions, you only have to walk down the street in this town – squillions of people like that – all moved down from London…"

I sit back up. "Is he giving any more talks?"

"Probably, at some point. Don't tell me you're going to start stalking Ossian Brohmer – like every other woman of a certain age in this town!"

"Why? Does he have some kind of fan club here?"

"He *lives* here."

"Ossian Brohmer lives *here*? In Quinton-on-Sea? Why didn't you tell me?"

Louis shrugs. "Sorry, darling, I didn't realise he was such a big nob. It's not like he's particularly well-known these days. He's just a fossil sitting in his crumbling Victorian pile. He doesn't really float my boat, to be honest."

"So… but where does he live, exactly?"

"Up on the cliff in the country park. In some strange tower – some Victorian folly. My friend Juliet's been there – apparently, it's filthy inside, full of dusty old furniture and cobwebs, like Miss Havisham lives there or something."

"I could go and rescue him!"

"I don't think he needs rescuing, Beanie. He has a steady supply of girlfriends, apparently. That's why Juliet got invited to dinner – she was a candidate, if you like – though I think Ossian's enthusiasm tailed off when he realised she was gay. He's a tosser, basically."

"Why are you so angry? Do you secretly fancy him or something?"

"Doesn't float my boat, not at all. But he treats

Quinton-on-Sea – when he's here, when he's not off on location, *darling*, or poncing around at film festivals – like a sweet shop. When he comes back here, he thinks he's the big fish in a small pond. He thinks every single woman in the vicinity is an item on display, just there for his delectation – even though he's this ancient fossil – before he waltzes off again. The problem is, in this town, the currency is arty-fartiness. So if you once made a semi-well-known film a billion years ago, that makes you incredibly important, and all these people, desperate for importance by association, go running after you. Actually, come to think of it, a woman *did* get done for stalking him. It was in the local *Gazette*."

"You see, it's women running after him, stalking him, not the other way round! Maybe I could be his cleaner or something. It sounds like he needs a cleaner."

"You don't want to go rummaging around Ossian Brohmer's dusty, hidden enclaves."

"But I do!"

"Don't tell me. You feel like you're *the one* who could understand him."

"But I do! I am!"

I picture Ossian Brohmer, like a fish out of water, in his gloomy Victorian folly. Displaced, in exile, when he should be next to a sparkling, clear Scandinavian lake, open to the northern sky. Next thing, for some reason, I'm picturing myself with Ossian Brohmer in a house full of natural light, clean lines and furniture of minimalist design, somewhere in Sweden. Then we're at the airport, carrying our bags through Arrivals – an image reminiscent of some paparazzi shot, then duplicated in some online tabloid – because, of course, there's the need to travel on location and to attend various international film festivals.

I come back to reality, back to the present moment, and stare at the photo of Ossian Brohmer. Not only is there a chance I might spot this god-like figure in Louis's backyard, so to speak, but finally I'm holding the Grail itself.

"Just knowing he lives quite close… it's quite mega, really."

"If you say so. I just worry about you, Beanie… getting carried away by fanciful ideas, sometimes. At the end of the day, he's hardly ever here."

"Okay! Just because I thought he might need a PA or a cleaner or something… No need to rain on my parade! Anyway…. Can we watch this *now*?"

"*Now*? I'm 'filmed out' for today, Beanie. Just watch it tomorrow when I'm at work."

"You're going to work on a Sunday?"

"Sure. Doing some viewings for the down-from-Londoners, then off to The Candy Box. It's good. You'll be able to relax, make yourself at home… undisturbed. I guess for you it's the equivalent of watching a porn film? The attraction of death. *Le grand mort* as opposed to *le petit mort*!"

I'm just about to slide the DVD back when I notice, tucked at the back of the shelf, a small clear plastic bag with tiny light blue pills in it. Surreptitiously, I pull it forward and see a little smiley face etched in the surface of one of the five tablets. I slide the bag back into its hideaway and re-shelve the DVD.

10

The Old Cinema at Yeotonville

Sunday.

Not only has the hot, sunny weather returned, but the town takes on a new significance as though it's been sprinkled with fairy dust overnight. I walk more self-consciously along the seafront's pink and white paving stones, casting my eyes from side to side. I feel like I have an inner radar that will spot him right away; a radar that will start pulsating just because he's within a ten-metre radius.

I have to keep my feet on the ground and remember what Louis said about Ossian spending most of his time in London or at various film festivals around the world. Although... Louis's friend Juliet did get invited to his cliff-top home... he must be here *sometimes*, often enough that he's become acquainted with some of the locals.

I haven't watched *The Index of Dreams* yet. I'm saving it for later in the day – after dark. It's not the kind of film you'd watch when the sun is pounding down outside. I relish the anticipation, like it's a great big juicy piece of chocolate cake to look forward to.

I decide to lie on the beach again, near the pier. Closing my eyes, I start drifting into a reverie, as before. But this time, instead of Simon Beresford, it's the face of Ossian that appears, unbidden, in the private cinema of my mind. There were whole years in the past, clusters of four of five years even, when *The Index* remained locked in the back drawer of my brain's filing cabinet. But now it's being opened again and again in quick succession by outward events, as though something has permanently shifted – something beyond my control, in the outer world; as though an ice-sheet has calved – a whole shelf of the Antarctic has broken loose and floated into warmer waters.

The first time I heard the name Ossian Brohmer, I was fourteen years old and *The Index of Dreams* had just been released in the cinema. When I heard that it was about suicide, I desperately wanted to go and see it, but it was Certificate 18. There was one girl in my class at school, Andrea Rosenhay, who was quite tall and 'well developed' for her age, i.e. she had a chest size of 36-C. She was quite a sensible, plain, boring girl in many ways, not someone I was particularly close to, and not really a rebel. But the thing was, she managed to do something quite naughty. She put on plenty of make-up and stood in the queue outside the old cinema in Yeotonville with her 17-year-old boyfriend and managed to get in to see *The Index of Dreams*. I was quite jealous and begged her for all the details. I can picture her now, ensconced on one of the old-fashioned, flip-top wooden desks in the classroom, sitting there in her blue school uniform, swinging her legs, looking confident, while a small group of us gathered around to hear about 'the must-see film of the moment'. She said it was about a mad scientist who had created an institute called The Index of Dreams where people could go and talk about suicidal feelings without anyone trying to 'cure' them. And, then, if they wanted, they could go ahead and take a suicide pill.

The Institute was so beautiful, though, that it could reawaken your appetite for life – but that was the conundrum, because then you'd have to go back to the 'real world' and get a job and so forth. Besides which, most people in the film were, apparently, just suicidal and just enjoyed all the luxury as a pleasant entrée to the main deal – the being able to just let go of everything and not worry about anything any more.

Some of the really serious depressives were so relieved to get to The Index of Dreams, they would arrive with tears in their eyes. They said they'd found their natural family, the people who could understand them; that it was like 'coming home' with such a sense of longing. One character described the feeling as, "a gentle explosion of seeds in her solar plexus."

"It sounds amazing!" I burst out.

Then this girl who was very cool, Carina Thomas,

laughed, "Keep your hair on, Beanie Upsell! It's only a film!"

"Yeah, it was no big deal," concurred Andrea Rosenhay, calmly.

Then Camilla Clothier, whose brother was born with spina bifida butted in. "Beanie Upsell, you make me sick! There are people out there who will never get the luxury of doing something as simple as walking, going on a mountain holiday, swimming in a lake, maybe never able to have children; they can't just…" – and here she made speech marks, wagging her index fingers – "'change their mind' and decide to get better. They don't have the luxury of that choice. I'm sorry, but you're just a bit sheltered from the harsh realities of life. For some people, just being able to walk down the street, dance at a disco, climb up a hill, would be pretty amazing, would make them feel ecstatic. I'm sorry, but being depressed is a luxury!"

I tried to keep my face buoyant-looking, but Camilla's remarks, her moral high-ground, her certainty, made me feel even more depressed.

"Beanie Upsell! You look really *down!*" shrieked Carina Thomas.

And then they started talking about something else.

One day, soon after Andrea Rosenhay had relayed all this to me, my parents were out for the whole day at some convention to do with antiques and this gave me the perfect opportunity to carry out a secret plan that had been evolving in my mind. I sneaked one of my mother's bras from her chest of drawers, then put it on and stuffed it with cotton wool (the reason I needed one of hers was because mine were only 32AA – more like a beginner bra for those who hadn't really grown anything yet). I stood in front of the mirror in her bathroom and helped myself to the full gamut of make-up. I wasn't quite sure what the toner was for – and I'm still not quite sure even now – but I dabbed some onto a ball of cotton wool anyway, and ran it firmly across both cheeks and my chin. Next, I put on the foundation (in a shade called 'Mystery'), then stretched my mouth wide and ran a hot-pink lipstick across my lower and upper lips. Briefly, I tried on a pair of stiletto heels, but I couldn't stand up straight in them, even when standing still, so I opted for my ankle boots which had a slight heel. I ditched my usual grunge-style jeans and floppy shirt combo for a tight-fitting fluffy jumper and a pair of black cords.

Inside, I was on fire with excitement. My stomach was a molten furnace of anticipation and fear. I took the bus to Yeotonville, ate fried egg and chips for lunch in a greasy spoon café, and then joined the queue at the cinema.

Finally, I got to the front of the queue for *The Index of Dreams*. Just staring at the giant poster, with its close-up of Stina and Albin, the lead characters, sharpened my longing to enter their world of beauty and release. Their complexions were fresh, alive, as though their blood shone through their delicate skin; their blonde hair was fine, like silk, with a glimmer of reddish gold under a pale sun. And, just visible in the background, with their icing of snow, you glimpsed the big wrought-iron gates that led to the institute – to the Index of Dreams.

I stood at the box office as though at the mouth to

Hades, my heart beating hard. The large array of chocolate bars and sweets – rows and rows of them – looked plastic, inedible, unreal. The only thing I needed was the passport to *The Index*.

"You're not 18," said the ticket seller – a formidable, middle-aged woman with a sour face and a 'take no prisoners' tone of voice. It felt like someone had just punched me in the stomach, or had denied me access to the only being I could ever love.

Smarting, winded, humiliated, I had no choice but to walk away. I had a sense of everyone else in the queue being in groups of two, three or more and I think I heard someone jeer as I headed back to the big glass swing doors and out into the daylight.

I was just taking a shortcut through the car park to get back to the bus station when I saw the fire-exit door opening at the back of the building. A youth wearing the *de rigueur* purple polyester waistcoat of the cinema staff appeared and proceeded to take a pack of Marlboro Lights out of his black polyester trousers and then lit a cigarette. He inhaled uncertainly, like he was practising smoking, like he'd only just started. I threaded my way back through the car park, towards the fire exit door, towards the boy. As I approached, he looked on nervously, as though I was about to accuse him of something.

And then it came to me, the line that I would say. I'd been at a party the week before where someone had thrown up as they were walking down the stairs and their vomit had landed on the head of a girl who was a couple of steps beneath him. So this girl with the vomit on her head, and her friend, waited in line outside the bathroom, desperate to get in. Everybody was complaining that a boy had been in there for over five minutes. What was he doing? The friend, who was very confident, marched to the front of the queue and rapped on the door. "If you don't open this door right now, I'm going to give you a blow job!" Miraculously, the door opened almost immediately after that and the boy emerged, looking sheepish. The confident girl laughed and took her vomit-strewn friend into the bathroom.

That's what gave me the idea. I wanted to be like the confident girl. Normally, I liked to be a goody-two-shoes, at least outwardly. It felt safer. It made life easier. But this felt like a matter of life or death. A life force, a wellspring, a necessity that could not be denied.

So I walked up to the boy and said, "You'd better let me past or I'm going to give you a blow job!"

And it worked. Like magic. He looked startled and stepped back, flattening himself against the door, making room for me to pass.

After film showings at Yeotonville Cinema they always let the audience out through the fire-exit doors (well, at least they did back then, in 1994, when the cinema still existed) so I knew it should be a breeze to walk in, and gain access through the doors at the bottom of the auditorium. Well, almost a breeze. My heart was beating fast. I was terrified that the woman with the sour face, the ticket seller, would be marching down the corridor for some reason. Maybe she'd be coming with one of those little torches to show all the latecomers to their seats. I kept my eyes on the swirly-patterned carpet, and kept walking up the gradient to the auditorium door.

Keep going. Keep breathing. Keep going.

Hey presto, I thought to myself, pushing open the swing door into the near darkness. I sat down in the middle of a row near the back, just to make sure I disappeared into the crowd.

In those days, they had these kind of diaphanous pink curtains across the stage that swung back and then the Pearl & Dean adverts would begin. Some of the adverts were clunky, like the one for a local Chinese restaurant and the local Volvo repair garage, but others held me in their sway. A beautiful woman with her hair in a bob dancing salsa in somewhere like Havana, all shot in black and white. She runs down a street, pursued by photographers. Advertising designer perfume. It made me long for a life less ordinary, to exist in another realm, to have glamour, be glamorous. Special.

Then there was an advert for Perrier water. A woman threw her head back, and the bottle was held aloft, pouring water into her open mouth like a fountain. It was then I realised how thirsty I was. Really thirsty after the adrenaline of sneaking in. Then the diaphanous curtains were closing with that Pearl & Dean music again, "Da-da, da-da, da-da, da-da, dadada…" And then the usherettes came in with their trays of ice-creams and fizzy drinks.

There was no sign of the sour-faced woman, and the lights were still low, so I went down the aisle to the front to get some water or maybe a Diet Coke. Then I could really relax for what was about to unfold. The secret. The dream. The ultimate. And that's when I saw her. The sour-faced ticket-seller. Or rather, she saw me. She was hovering by the exit door with her little spy torch.

Perhaps looking out for me. And then she was advancing towards me, taking my arm, leading me to the exit, just as they were beginning to play the theme music of *The Index* through the loudspeakers. The melancholy music receded as she frog-marched me up the swirly-carpeted-gradient and then faded away altogether as she man-handled me through another set of swing doors that led to the foyer.

The woman expelled me firmly, back through the main entrance, back into the harsh light of day. Lucky that she wasn't calling my parents, lucky that she wasn't calling the police, blah, blah, blah, and all that kind of thing.

Still in shock at my daring (and terrified that someone who recognised me might have witnessed the incident), I went into the nearest public toilets and took off the bra, threw the cotton wool in the bin, washed the make-up off and stared at my pale, glum face in the mirror. Despite the fear and aftermath of trying to get into the cinema, I quickly hatched another plan. When the film came out on video, I'd ask Andrea Rosenhay to slap on a load of makeup and go and rent a copy from Blockbusters for me. The only problem was, about two weeks later, some parent, somewhere, blamed *The Index of Dreams* on their daughter's suicide. And then it was banned.

Later that year I used my Christmas money to buy Ossian Brohmer's autobiography *After Dark,* and one day my stepdad marches into my room, sees the book on the floor and says, "I don't want that book in this house! That man's a heroin addict!"

So I said, "He's not any more!"

Anyway, my stepdad had this way of speaking that always reduced me to tears; it made me feel really scared. And then he took the book, tore it up and threw it on the fire in the sitting room, saying, "That's the end of that!"

Not only had my reading of Ossian Brohmer's life been cut short – I'd only got to chapter two, chronicling his teenage years in the coastal town of Marstrand (which influenced his setting for the Institute in *The Index*) – but it was as if my own life had also been interrupted, its life blood cut off, denied.

I'd shut myself in the bathroom, as that was the only room in the house with a lock on it, and dug my nails into my skin until it was damaged. I picked up a razor, but I didn't like the idea of blood. That was why Ossian understood me. He knew about death wishes, but he understood that people didn't want to die alone, violently. I stood in front of the mirror, in front of my scratched face, and prayed to God that somehow I could meet Ossian, even though he lived far away, in another country. Somehow, somehow, I just had to meet him. I wanted to walk under a northern sky with him, to walk through beautiful, crystalline snow with him by my side.

And that was the moment I put everything to do with *The Index* into a drawer – a drawer tucked away in the back of my mind, and locked it firmly shut. Maybe, one day, I might bring it back out. If I survived that long. Because, like the characters in the film, I wasn't sure just how long I planned to stick around.

I must have fallen asleep. I look around at the near-deserted beach. It's not dark yet, but it's nearly time – time to watch *The Index of Dreams*.

11

The Index of Dreams

Even if worm-holes are one day proven not to exist – I don't mean worm-holes in the ground, but the worm-holes in Einstein's Theory of Relativity that indicate the possibility of some kind of time-space travel… the thing is, the power of the imagination alone can take one back to the past so vividly that it's like a living dream: A place that is shrouded in emotion, pure aesthetics… I'm living it here and now as I enter this other world. A world of the senses where life begins to beat again.

The opening sequence hits me in a visceral way. The melancholy piano music of the score is familiar, not only because I'd heard it briefly during my little escapade in Yeotonville Cinema all those years ago and, years later, rediscovered it on YouTube, but also it had continued to pop up intermittently on TV whenever there was a debate about death, euthanasia or teenagers self-harming, etc.

The main character, Stina, is trapped in her room, studying and studying. Her parents tell her that one day life will begin, when she's an adult, when she leaves home. But even before the day to leave comes, something dies inside her. She stands in the hallway of the family home, vis-à-vis her parents.

A whisper goes around certain circles in the sixth form, in the more punky circles – they're talking about a place called The Index of Dreams where you can die a painless death. Nobody knows where it is. The newspapers are banned from talking about it. But apparently some depressed people have started a secret network of information about how to get to there. Somebody says it might be in the mountains of Switzerland, but nobody knows for sure. Another school friend says that all you have to do is wait at a certain place, at a certain time, at Gothenburg Central Station and someone will come to collect you and take you to the Institute, which is very beautiful, in a countryside location.

Stina's classmate, Albin, is in love with her. What can he do to win her love? There is one thing, she says. He has to find out how to get to the Index of Dreams. One day, Albin runs into the forest to find her. He has the information, but he doesn't want to give it to her, of course. Suddenly, Stina feels alive again at the thought of gaining the secret code, of going on this adventure.

"I'll give it to you only on the condition that you come back," says Albin.

Stina touches his hand. "I don't think death is the end. It's just a journey to somewhere else, away from this horrible world. I feel excited that I could make this transition without pain, fear or loneliness."

As a compromise, she allows Albin to go with her to The Index. As long as he's with her, he thinks, he can persuade her to come back, to stay on planet Earth, to be loved. But Albin has underestimated her determination; it's as though some ineradicable message is there, in her DNA...

They wait at Gothenburg Station, at the appointed place, near a telephone kiosk, and Stina smiles with a sense of recognition, bonding with the other people who are also waiting there. At 5pm a distinguished-looking, middle-aged man arrives and greets each one in turn, shaking their hands.

"You're here for the special departure?" asks the man.

The teenagers nod, a little nervously, but you can sense the keen anticipation in all of them – or almost all of them.

"My name is Dr Nordholm. Follow me – except you." He senses that Albin is not 'one of them.' "I'm afraid you'll have to stay here. It's not your time," he tells him.

As they follow the man out of the station, Albin calls after her, "Stina! Stina! Just remember to come back! I'll look after you!"

"Please don't shout! I'm fine! I'll be in touch." She quickly turns away and remarks to one of her fellow travellers, Loke, that Dr Nordholm has the sombre stillness of a judge.

"He has no agenda. He's not trying to make anybody do anything. He only wants to facilitate – to facilitate the outcome that we want," she whispers.

They travel by minibus in the dark to the unknown location. It's a long journey. At the gates to the institute, Dr Nordholm leans towards a security camera to announce their arrival. A lock mechanism is released and the gates swing open. The minibus continues up the drive to a large turreted building, reminiscent of a medieval castle.

A steward greets them in the warm foyer. While the teenagers are settling into their rooms, a maid arrives to take their meal requests. As it's the run-up to the 'ultimate departure', it's a special time. No request is too much. Whether lobster, a perfectly ripe mango or perfectly ripe strawberries – champagne, even – everything is available.

After the banquet the teenagers gather in the main hall, where logs burn brightly in the giant fireplace. Stina quickly forms a special friendship with Loke.

The youths sit in window-seats, or cross-legged on the floor, while Dr Nordholm introduces the concept of The Index of Dreams "…Unfettered by a history of taboo around suicide, life is just an energy. If we feel our programming is irreparably faulty, we have the right to transform our energy – to begin again in a new form."

The 'Indexers' share their stories of childhood trauma. Witnessing a parent's suicide. A stillborn sibling. Sexual abuse. A chronic illness, which still causes extreme pain. A general malaise and depression without being sure why. They've tried to see the light at the end of the tunnel, but it feels more of a relief to admit that what they'd really like to do is 'transit'.

Then there's a sharing of more wide-ranging ideas about life and death. What they mean. Where we're from. Where we return to. Whether we'll be reincarnated. Whether life will continue to exist on planet Earth as we know it, or whether there will be mass extinctions, environmental catastrophe in their lifetime (if they were to stay). Or, even, whether someone will press the nuclear button and blow the planet up.

One girl believes humans were created by extra-terrestrials as an experiment, but that the experiment went wrong. We were supposed to enjoy life as pure bliss, but in a physical, as opposed to a spiritual form (the spirit world is our origin); but something went awry, and the unintended elements of aggression and cruelty got out of hand. Because humans fall in love – the passionate, loving element is there, too – they can't help but reproduce, but with all the risks and tragedies that come with that. Anyway, once the extra terrestrials realised their experiment had gone wrong, they left – left us to it – and zoomed back to wherever they came from, another planet light years away.

It's 2am by the time most of them head to bed. The teenagers embrace one another, like a new-found family. Exhausted, happy, understood – excited, even.

The next day Stina spends time with Loke: swimming in the spa pool, followed by a hot stone therapy treatment, then cycling around the grounds. Free of social norms, they talk endlessly about all the times they fantasised about taking a painless suicide pill.

There's a special workshop for the very depressed individuals who feel unloved and unable to socialise. Their depression has paralysed them, to the point they want to just lie on their beds and wait to be brought the special euthanasia pill. But they have the choice of the special workshop – to try and have a breakthrough moment before the ultimate departure. Stina, and some of the other more sociable ones, attend in order to give moral support, in order that those on a 'knife edge' don't feel so isolated.

On day three, she and Loke cycle around the beautiful grounds again, around a huge lake, before their 'aroma-therapy' workshop. You can choose the incense you would like burning as you pass away to the fourth dimension. They experiment with essential oils and incense crystals until they find their ideal combination. Stina has a special memory of lavender fields in Provence and has no hesitation in choosing essence of lavender, blended with a trace of frankincense. Loke chooses a traditional Japanese-based mixture of cinnamon, clove, sandalwood and spices.

It's during the workshop that Loke plucks up the courage to propose to Stina: "Would you like to transit together? Holding hands?"

Stina is moved by the suggestion. "Even though we're near the end, so nothing should matter... it matters just as much, doesn't it? To not feel alone. That's what I've always wanted – to not feel alone."

On the fourth day, two of the 'Indexers' feel so revived by their stay at the institute that they want to go back to life outside. Dr Nordholm has already spoken about this possi-bility: that the special time can restore people's appetite for life – so much so that they're ready to 'rejoin the fray.' Of course, it's a conundrum because they'll have to face all the issues that once drove them here: exam pressure, getting a job, financial worries in the future, the state of the environment. But free will is everything and the 'exiters' get driven in the minibus back to Gothenburg Station. Dr Nordholm explains that in some ways the effect of The Index is counterintuitive – the knowledge that we have the choice to end our life at a time of our choosing, painlessly, can provoke life itself. It means that, on reflection, we might choose to stay longer, because now we feel safe. In the modern world, he explains, people are forced into the 'numbers game' – quantity, but not necessarily quality, of life.

Also on day four, Stina and Loke attend a festive party for those whose 'transition' is imminent. There is a list – an index, if you like – of the special things you might choose to do. It doesn't have to be party. It might be a group meditation, for example. Or a one-to-one counselling session. But it's the festive party that Stina and Loke have chosen. They take a special potion that contains an MDMA-type substance, and dance until dawn. About fifty of the Indexers have chosen the party. It feels like New Year's Eve but intensified by a factor of ten.

On day five, Stina telephones Albin to say goodbye. He tries to persuade her to stay, but Stina hangs up.

Stina and Loke enter the darkened chamber. You just see their backs as they disappear into a cloud of incense. In the very final shot, they're lying side by side, holding hands, like medieval effigies carved in stone, their faces turned up to the heavens.

Last night, after watching the film, I had a strange dream. I was standing with Ossian outside the gates of The Index. The gates, as I remembered them from the film – and from the cinema poster all those years ago – were fairly large; but in the phantasmagoria of the dream they stretched like giants into the sky: ornamental, wrought iron with elegant curlicues, arabesques, and, towards the top, gold-leaf ornaments. We stood like pygmies, staring through the spirals at the drive that stretched onwards and onwards. Ancient palm trees punctuated the smooth green lawns; they disdained the ground, only deigning to unfurl their fan-shaped leaves much nearer the sky.

For some reason, in my dreamscape, The Index of Dreams was in this exotic country. It felt tropical, with its large forest of banyan roots tumbling in strange, contorted shapes. As for the institute itself, you couldn't see it at all, except for an edge of white – like the solid white edge of a wedding cake – through a gap in the extravagant vegetation.

In the dream, the Institute belonged to the past and now it was just a private home. A sense of desertion was there because its super-rich owner – probably a Russian oligarch or someone like that – was out of town.

And then the phantasmagoria of the scene became confused with Manderley in the opening scene of *Rebecca*, except that, unlike the narrator in *Rebecca*, I couldn't fly through the gates, and even Ossisan Brohmer was locked out, like a little pygmy staring longingly back at some past decade that had turned into an image, some lost *belle epoque* that could never be touched again.

And then scenes of London tumbled towards me. Red buses. People spilling out of crowded trains. Then I'm in an aeroplane that can't land on the frozen tundra below.

I wake up, disturbed by the images. I need to get a grip. Perhaps I need to make some changes. Perhaps it's time to make a fresh start.

※

Louis emerges from his room, rubbing his eyes.

"It's a shame you didn't come to the Candy Box last night! It was rocking! D J Topsie Smith spinning some wicked tunes… At least you watched the film in the *evening*, not wrapped up like some recluse on a sunny day in front of the box. In fact, Beanie, I get a feeling you've changed incrementally in some way. Like a speck of sun breaking through into a dark room! So… anyway, how *was* the film?"

"Mm, amazing! Brilliant! Really, *really* amazing. It feels like a missing piece in my life is now in place. Do you know what I mean?"

"Not *quite.*"

"But the thing is, I had a weird dream last night. I was standing with Ossian Brohmer outside the gates of The Index of Dreams. Sort of locked out. A really off-the-wall dream. What do you think it meant?"

"What it says on the can, Beanie. Locked out… a fantasy…that kind of thing…"

"It doesn't have to be!"

"It means leave the past behind. Look, I'll make some cappuccinos and we can sit out on the balcony."

I lean on the kitchen door jamb and watch Louis as he sets to work on his buffed chrome machine with fancy, curved edges.

"You have to have a good quality bean. Filtered

water. It's all about creating the resistance as the steam encounters the packed espresso... the steam is forced through... it takes a few moments to get going... then it starts dripping with this thick, honey-like density... like so... Then the secret with the milk is the size of the bubbles. They have to be very, very small."

I watch as Louis holds a metal jug of milk at an angle under the steam wand. He removes the metal jug, checks, then holds it towards me.

"See. The bubbles are still too big."

He holds the jug under the steam wand again, moving it gently from side to side, then tests the temperature of the jug with his hand.

"About 60°. So now I pour this velvety milk onto the espresso. Perfect."

Louis has something that looks like a pen marker, but in fact it's full of liquid chocolate. He carefully rotates the 'pen' over the milk, creating two delicate circles.

"Wow! It's worth coming here just for *this* alone! Thanks, Louis!"

We take our cappuccinos onto the balcony and install ourselves on the white, wrought iron chairs, in the full sun.

"So, the big question, Beanie, is what are you going to do now?"

"Now? Before I get the train?"

"No. Generally. With your life. Because the thing is, you need to move out of these obsessions... I always knew you liked to be fanciful, but this fetish about *Index of Dreams*, for example..."

"But apart from things like your cappuccino, there isn't a lot that really grabs me in life…"

"The thing about obsessions, Beanie, when you've got a craze about somebody like Ossian Brohmer, it represents something you're suppressing. The thing you're not owning in yourself… you see it in someone else. So Ossian Brohmer, he symbolises your suppressed creativity. Perhaps *you* would like to make a film?"

"*Me*?"

"Yes. *You*."

"Don't be crazy!"

"Sign up for a film course… buy a digital camera for a couple of hundred… experiment… make a short film… it's all *do-able*."

"*Me? Don't be *crazy*!"

Louis stands on the platform, waving goodbye as the train pulls out of the station and I register, with satisfaction, that I've actually *been away* for the Bank Holiday. An enjoyable Bank Holiday. And, whatever my previous misgivings about Quinton-on-Sea, I concede that it must be a place of significance if a *certain person* lives there. Cosmopolitan. On the map. And not just *any* film director. But 'OB' himself. Since Louis's lecture, I'm a little more self-conscious about my obsession. So I skim over the name quickly, as though it's just a hazy, unspecified thought.

And then the part about projecting – taking

'ownership' of my creativity. Maybe Louis's been listening to one too many motivational speakers. Then again, maybe I *could* check on-line and look at film schools. Just a short course. An experiment. Beanie Upsell, walking into a film school. The idea does seem fanciful, though. *Even more* fanciful than my reveries about bumping into 'OB'.

12

Sea Change

But I think something *might* have shifted since my visit to Quinton-on-Sea.

There are other places in the world besides Lewisham. Besides London. I ring an agency – not the temping agency, but an estate agency. I'd like to have my one-bed flat valued. The estate agents clamour to my door, all big smiles and enthusiasm. It's nice being the one in charge. It's nice being the customer. And it's even nicer to know that your unassuming flat, which is located in an area that you don't find totally inspiring, will sell like a hot cake for £200,000.

I glimpse the possibility of a new life. If I'm strategic with the equity of £110,000, perhaps I can buy somewhere outright and become semi-independent of 'the system' – perhaps retrain; perhaps never work as a secretary ever again! The sense of relief feels like sun breaking out from behind a cloud; it feels like a suit of armour dropping away from my body. It feels like perhaps we could have evolved on the planet, over the millennia, for a reason; that life is wanting to live. I can't say I feel it *totally* yet, but I feel like I can breathe.

Each morning I wake up and Google property websites in towns that sound quite groovy: Southwold-on-Sea, Hebden Bridge, Totnes. I find myself peering, from hundreds of miles away, into the bedrooms, bathrooms and kitchens of total strangers, wondering if theirs is a house I would like to live in. I press the 'Street View' button and find myself dabbing the cursor with my finger, looking further down the virtual road to see what's going on in the area. Then I can't get the cursor to go in the right direction, it spins round and ends up against a blurry signpost. I see strangers carrying their shopping in plastic bags, freeze-framed by the camera, their faces pixelated, and suddenly I click off the whole thing, feeling sucked into too much virtual reality. It's when night falls that the doubts set in. It's like sticking a pin in a map. I don't actually *know* anyone in Southwold-on-Sea, Hebden Bridge or Totnes. There's always Quinton-on-Sea. But would I be moving there just because 'OB' is occasionally in residence? I need to prove, to both myself and Louis that I'm not moving somewhere based on a fantasy. I stare out at the dark of the night sky and feel afraid. I don't actually know where I'm going.

I ring Louis.

"Well, you've called the right person. I *am* an estate agent, darling. How about Quinton for a while? Just to give yourself time to think about things. It would be a terrific idea for you to come back here. You could stay in my spare room again, if you need to. Or I could help you find somewhere to rent."

"I'm not sure…"

"It's totally up-and-coming here, darling. There's so much going on. And you'll still be reasonably near London. You don't want to live *too* far away from London until you've followed up with 'you know who'…"

"Who? You mean the guy I spoke to for five minutes at the law firm? I don't *think* so!"

"And you haven't even been to The Candy Box yet. There's so much going on at The Candy Box. It's just a fun place to go. There are so many cool people here. Oh, yes, I forgot to tell you, your other love interest was sitting at the next table to me in The Coffee Cabin yesterday."

"What do you mean, 'my other love interest'?"

"Ossian Brohmer, darling!"

I 3

Edgy

I'm here to meet Mark, the estate agent from Pukka Properties. Louis is away on holiday in Barcelona, but I've done a little bit of research by myself and found some prospective rentals – just with a view to treading water for six months until I know for sure where to start my new life. And what I should *do* with my new life.

Mark is waiting in the doorway of 2, The Promenade, standing next to a pile of black rubbish bags and a discarded mattress.

"Beanie? Mark!" he says, shaking my hand with a firm grip. "Sorry about the mess. It's quite edgy around here. But it's a lovely flat inside."

The building is very, very tall and the six buzzers indicate the number of units within.

"Okay. Let's do the business!" Mark has his keys at the ready but as he tries to insert the Yale key, the door swings open. A threadbare blue carpet covers the hallway where unopened junk mail litters the floor.

"Are you a DFL?" asks Mark as I climb after his pinstriped suit up the stairs.

"Sorry?"

"A Down from Londoner."

"Kind of – though I was born in Bath."

"That's not just up-and-coming, is it? It's sort of been 'up' for a long time – Jane Austen and all that."

We pass an abandoned television and a broken toy pushchair on the landing.

"Oh, do excuse the... round here, things can be a little more Tracey Emin than Jane Austen. That's what appeals to some of the DFLs, though. They don't want things too perfect, if you know what I mean."

"Like, who wants to live in a chocolate box village?"

"Exactly. I have to admit, the approach is a little like The No Star Hotel, Bangkok, but..." Mark inserts the key into the lock, "...the flat itself is a steal at £400 per calendar month."

I have an instinct that I shouldn't take the flat even before he's opened the inner door. Once inside, however, I try to see the positives: the scale of the rooms, the high ceilings, the sea views. Perhaps it's a little like Louis's flat? I have to admit, it isn't *quite*. The days of snaffling up an up-market Art Deco flat for £35,000, or £300 a month, are ancient history, really.

"Original features everywhere, of course," says Mark, pointing to the cornice and then the fireplace. "Brand new kitchen! Newly-fitted bathroom."

The current occupiers have sumptuous furniture in situ: vintage leather sofas, a mid-century Scandinavian daybed and an up-cycled dining table with the top painted in a shade of grey that's probably called something like 'stone' or 'oyster'.

"Why are they moving?" I ask.

"Totally valid reasons. They're recently married, expecting a baby and moving nearer to her parents in the West Country. Buying a new-build – somewhere like Wincanton."

I feel a stab of regret that it's not me who's moving to the West Country, even if it is only Wincanton. But, the fact is, I don't know anyone in the West Country any more.

I stand at the window, looking out to sea. "I think I'll take it."

Back in Lewisham, in between packing, I lie in bed and sleep a lot. For some reason, Simon Beresford keeps appearing in my mind. And, for some reason, I keep pondering the fact that I'm moving away from London, where Simon Beresford lives. Or does he? I don't know where he lives *exactly*, but I'm hardly going to bump into him in a scruffy seaside town. But, then again, I stand a chance of running into 'OB' in Quinton-on-Sea, or at least seeing him from afar.

This is crazy – as though I could be basing my decision around (i) a man who doesn't even know I exist and, even if he did, I imagine him looking at me with that expression of Nordic disdain; or (ii) a man who I've only met briefly and who may have no interest in seeing me ever again. Besides which, if I'd wanted the certainty of seeing Simon Beresford every single day of the week (or, at least, five days a week) then I could have taken up Slim Pickings' offer and become a secretary – or legal

support, whatever they wanted to call it – at Worley &
Beresford. Though it's hardly as though I, Beanie Upsell,
would be a good candidate for any man that more sorted
women would also find attractive. Or, if I did stand a
chance, my lack of normality would come to light sooner
or later... although maybe I *am* more normal now? I'm
not quite sure.

14

Vintage Gothic
Romance

My flat does sell like a hot cake and, just in time to catch the end of summer, I'm now living in up-and-coming Quinton-on-Sea, in the converted, once-grand, Victorian house. My insubstantial furniture looks small, like dolls-house furniture in the vast rooms. It doesn't look quite as lovely as when the previous occupiers lived here, with their expensive, retro pieces. I'd been attracted by the fact it was good value, in terms of price per square metre, but now I'm starting to feel I made a mistake. At night, there's the clanking sound, at regular intervals, of some old boiler and a gassy smell pervades the stairway – and even the inside of my flat.

I look out the window at the expanse of sea and a large grey liner on the horizon, which resembles a warship. The sound of the crashing waves, which I can hear without even leaving my front door, still can't clear this undertow that has taken me over, especially now the initial burst of sun and optimism in May, the feeling of holiday, is just a memory.

I had thought the faded Victorian grandeur might suit my mood of disappearing into the woodwork, of living between the cracks, for a while. But now I'm not so sure. There's something about the way the town's large villas are divided into bedsits, the way the refuse sacks pile up on rubbish day, together with the odd discarded fridge or washing machine, that's a bit depressing. Scavenging seagulls peck open the black plastic bags, leaving a trail of cotton buds, nappies, chicken bones and discarded food packaging down the street.

The neighbouring, derelict hotel has a slightly sinister atmosphere, with its boarded-up windows, particularly at night. A traffic cone is regularly placed on the head of the statue of Queen Victoria, an edifice placed in the most prominent square by those once affluent citizens, the optimistic Victorians. Sometimes I feel there are ghosts haunting their pleasure-dome that once was – with its flotsam and jetsam and the odd discarded syringe – with a sense of incredulity; like days of reckoning long after their departure; a reckoning for trade routes bringing cheap sugar and opium, and now cocaine, rendering the citizens weak; something rotten at the core, working its way to the surface.

The weather continues its overcast mood, and I spend a rainy morning cogitating in a bookshop café, pondering all the directions I could take: an art course, a writing course, an aromatherapy course – a personal development course? I could give myself six months off, using my squirrelled-away money... take a course to retrain... a new career... the film course, even, that Louis mentioned?

A plump woman in a vintage dress, with a slick of bright-red lipstick on her mouth, orders a latte and joins her companion – a small man wearing black jeans, a T-shirt and a pork-pie hat – on the shabby chic sofa. She talks in an over-excited, loud voice about a private view she's attending, as though she's conscious of everyone listening, and then lowers her voice as she switches to more gossipy matters, but still loud enough for me to hear snatches. "Well, I heard it's falling to pieces... Grade II listed... don't know if he can afford the upkeep. I don't know if he's still knocking around with... well, why would he, when... his girlfriend... young, beautiful, rich... Naomi... so Sarah said... no, no, it was Gaby Smith... she said... I know... I know... he made it clear it was just a one-night stand. Well, of course, when *I* got invited there... yes, I know, I know... no... no... *very* private."

And then the man in the pork pie hat says something like, "He might be a bit strange but everyone wants the chance to add him on Facebook."

And then the plump 'vintage' woman says, "*Ossian Brohmer* on Facebook? Well, he wasn't on there the *last time* I checked!"

My ears literally tingle, alert, but the 'vintage' woman's voice trails off momentarily as another woman in a fifties dress enters the café; then she bursts forth once more, "Darling! O.M.G.! What are *you* doing back? I thought you were still in London!!" She stands up and embraces the woman who's just arrived, air-kissing her on each cheek, "Mwah! Mwah!"

I trawl through the shelves of books – the plump 'vintage' woman's voice gabbling in the background now about exhibitions and private views – and peruse the cover of a fifties' Gothic romance, *The Web of Evil* by Lucille Emerick. A woman in a crimson, off-the-shoulder evening gown runs through the night, away from a foreboding looking house. Even in her flurry, though, she's caught, freeze-framed like a mannequin in an elegant pose. Across the top is the strap-line: *The story of a woman trapped by love.* I wonder if I feel tempted to read it and whether I could transpose myself into the role of the heroine, and pretend I'm enslaved by love for 'OB'. It's harder to imagine now. Now that I've overheard the 'vintage' woman talking about "…girlfriend… young, rich, beautiful…"

Anyway, I can't imagine myself wearing a crimson, off-the-shoulder evening gown… although I *could* easily imagine running away from a foreboding looking house in the middle of the night and the thrill of the escape. Still, I think, putting it back down, maybe I'll leave it for another time. There are a few more of them in the same ilk, and one of them is bound to still be here next time I visit.

In the end, I plump for a copy of *Mankind in Amnesia* by Immanuel Velikovsky. It's all about how mankind is subconsciously living a destructive lifestyle because we have a collective memory from a time when the Earth was hit by a giant meteorite that practically destroyed everyone and everything. And in the same way that people subconsciously recreate a traumatic past event because subconsciously they're trying to resolve it, so we're imprinted by this collective memory towards self-destruction because of the giant meteorite.

15

Amnesia

I find myself drifting towards the beach for no particular reason, feeling a bit shell-shocked.

I sit on the pebbles, looking at the horizon, and try to recall the 'vintage' woman's exact words. "Girlfriend... Young, rich, beautiful..." It feels like a slap, bringing me back to reality. I feel silly. Silly for thinking that Beanie Upsell might wend her way into Ossian Brohmer's life... those hazy, subliminal thoughts of 'hanging out', working on location, perhaps even a few PA duties... Because Louis had 'downgraded' Ossian's desirability by calling him a fossil who'd only ever made one film, I'd thought there might be a way of getting to know him. Like he was abandoned up there on the cliff top. Far from the madding crowd. I picture Ossian enamoured with his confident girlfriend, lounging around his house... helping out on set. I have to admit it; I've been deluding myself.

Suddenly, I'm not at all sure why I've even moved

here. I try to think it through logically. At some level –
subliminally, perhaps – I had been hoping a modicum
of involvement with Ossian would resolve my 'lifestyle'/
work, as well as any existential issue. Being his PA.
Going on location. At least in London I had structure
– the expectation to join the full-to-bursting compartments on the train, sit in an office for 8 hours, and then
wend my way back home – and no room for hope and its
twin of delusion. Here I feel the opposite. Like it would
be abnormal to be a nine-to-fiver. Like I'm supposed
to sit in coffee shops, planning my next art exhibition
or screenplay or whatever. Except I'm not an artist or
a writer. I've never created *anything*, actually. A blank
page. A hard place from which to start.

I stand back up, wobbly, scared that I'll go slightly
insane without a routine. Still in a fuggy state, I'm
walking past the amusement arcade, with its mad
cacophony blaring out a 'tune' that sounds like 'Oh my
darling, oh my darling Clementine!' A girl in a track-
suit stands on a rubber platform, performing aerobic
movements according to the instructions on a screen
in front of her. Other screens feature racing tracks. A
man in a 'driver's' seat concentrates, rapidly turning a
steering wheel this way and that, as he participates in
an imaginary Formula 1.

Keen to leave the noise behind, I hurry on, down
through an underpass and into the shopping precinct,
where I start looking in windows for no particular reason.
Now I'm staring at a shop-front with the words 'Office
Sprites Recruitment Agency' emblazoned across it.
Maybe it's some subconscious desire to self-destruct – or
to regain some kind of control over my life – a routine,

anything – but I actually walk in, and a woman called Belinda Dixey makes an appointment for me to register in one hour's time. They need some ID, so I head back to the flat, print out my CV, collect my passport and driving licence and go back to Office Sprites, contemplating that the only use I have for my travel documents these days – or have ever had – seems to be in my application for office roles, grounding myself rather than driving, sailing or flying.

The woman on reception efficiently ticks me off in the appointment book. I observe the white crispness of her blouse and the perfection of the way she has done her make-up and hair, as though I need to start re-absorbing the culture and the unwritten rules of appearance, commitment and conviction.

"Did you bring your ID? Wonderful. Is this your *current* driving licence?" The receptionist is carefully unfolding my frayed paper licence and studying it as though it's an ancient parchment. "Oh, don't worry, if you've got your passport. Perfect."

I have to wait a minute while she makes photocopies. Then I have the usual kind of speed-typing test, the content of which is the usual kind of absurd corporate-speak (this one, for example, is about the suntan lotion industry) that makes you want to vomit and every cell in your body starts screaming at you to get the hell out. As usual, though, I go through with it; the reminder of how much I hate being in this situation just makes me type faster and faster, as though the speed is the speed of running away. Of course it has the opposite effect because when the receptionist prints out my score she raises her eyebrows and says, "Not bad!" as a kind of understatement. Then I'm given a psychometric test, which I haven't ever had to do before. I'm given various hypothetical situations about dealing with various work dilemmas/people interactions and a range of options to tick about how I'd deal with it. They all look like trick questions so I just circle my options at random.

Then I'm interviewed by Belinda Dixey. I'm feeling a little over-confident, or diffident. After all, this is only Quinton-on-Sea, and I'm used to working in London. Belinda, after introducing herself, says straight out in a considered, matter-of-fact way, "Why do you want to be a secretary? You don't look like a secretary."

"I just want to temp."

"You don't look like a temporary secretary, even."

I feel both disarmed and caught out, in a way that is momentarily pleasing and liberating; for a few seconds, I find it hard to roll out the usual patina of words. That I don't look intrinsically like a secretary must be a good thing. I don't like the way secretaries are 'supposed' to look. Of course, I've always pretended. I've got very good at pretending, at being a robot secretary that knows how to please. I'm impressed by Belinda Dixey's calmness, her centredness, her ability to 'read' a person, her ability to see that I'm not a secretary.

I'm not quite sure *who* I am instead. I used to know – a long time ago – but I don't know any more. Perhaps that's the problem. But just for a moment, I have that glimpse, once more, of a life where I'm not a secretary, where I never go back to this, to an office. A life that feels completely free. And it's a good thing that Belinda thinks I don't look like a secretary. Perhaps it's her way of blowing me out, releasing me from this trap I've just sleepwalked into.

But then she says, "Are you used to handling confidential information?"

"Yes," I say. "I've worked for some quite high-profile people. I'm totally trustworthy. If I'd wanted to sell juicy scandal or blow whistles, I could have made money by now selling a few lurid stories. I once worked for a politician, a well-known figure who was often in the Sunday supplements with his blog; he just also happened to be a cocaine-addict."

At this point Belinda begins looking down at my CV again, studying it with some interest.

"Oh," I add hurriedly, "he's not on my CV; I resigned quite quickly because of his erratic behaviour. And that's just one of about five potential stories I have but which, beyond a shadow of a doubt, will stay in the realms of confidentiality. There but for the grace of God go I," I continue, "because we've all done things that we wouldn't want someone to film and put on YouTube. We've all done something embarrassing or wrong at some point in our lives; it's just most of us have got by without some screaming headline posted above a photo of it."

Belinda's eyes are actually quite wide at this point and then I know I'm way off track. I have an idea that this is my problem in life. I need to be more discreet. I need to learn what's *appropriate*. I think I might have really blown it now but Belinda, apart from her momentarily widened eyes, seems quite unperturbed, and simply adds, "Don't worry about all that. It's just the local police station urgently needs someone to transcribe a backlog of interviews and witness statements. Just for one week. Would you be interested in doing that?"

"Yes."

"And you'd be okay with signing the Official Secrets Act? They'll be able to explain it all to you."

"Yes."

"And would you be available to start next Monday at 9am?"

"Yes!"

"That's super, Sabina. I'll get your CV off to them right now."

"What are you up to?" asks Louis. "It's summer and you seem to be hibernating."

"I'm not actually. I'm going to be temping at the police station next week. Transcribing."

"Temping? What about your new start? Change of direction?"

"I was drifting... drifting out to sea. Thought I needed some structure. It's only a week."

"Just don't lose sight of the *main deal* in life, that's all. Take a risk. Do something risqué! Still... I guess... the police station, darling! You'll be able to fill me in on the seedy underworld of this town!"

"It's confidential. I'll be signing the Official Secrets Act."

"I'm jealous! You'll find out about all kinds of things... the shadow side, the underbelly, all the things that people want to keep in the dark."

"It's just a job, a typing job."

"If you say so. Anyway, what are you up to *today?*"

"I'm reading. I picked up this book, *Mankind in Amnesia*, in the Old Town. It says we're all doomed because the human race is recreating the trauma of a giant meteorite hitting the planet. Or, if we were aware of the subconscious trauma, and the reasons for it, then we could do something about it."

"Well, maybe, but it doesn't mean you have to bury yourself away in your flat. You need to get out more... There's a gang of us meeting down at The Candy Box tonight. And then there's a gig at Uncle Tom's Cabin. My Favourite Biscuit are playing."

"Who's My Favourite Biscuit?"

"They're an amazingly cool, indie folk band. How about it? There's this woman called Juliet..."

"The one who's been to Ossian Brohmer's house?"

"The very same. You'd really like her, Beanie. I just think it's important to discover yourself, whatever it takes. How can you reach 35 and never have experienced *le petit mort?*"

"I have actually."

"When! You didn't tell me! Who with?"

"No one."

"With yourself?"

"I was just *thinking* about someone. Lying on the beach and *thinking* about someone."

"You touched yourself on the beach?"

"It didn't involve any touching. I was just *imagining*."

"By just *imagining?* You're making it up."

"I'm not. Anyway. About this meteorite... maybe that's why the human race is destroying the planet, it's trying to recreate the trauma from this unresolved collective memory. Some people say we'll be extinct by 2035. Have you noticed how they keep pushing the date back? They used to say the world would end by 2000, then 2012, and now it's by 2035, or 2100 at the very latest."

"Well, with that kind of uncertainty, you might just as well get out there and go crazy, Beanie!"

"I was just feeling in a kind of slump, that's all. Maybe I could come round and watch *The Index of Dreams* again? I love that title, like you could just go through a list and choose your dream, choose your reality, and then you die."

"But that's what life actually is, Beanie. You try to live your dream, choose your reality, and then you die. It doesn't have to be a film."

16

A Great Aunt in Quinton

I decide to have a nap and then I decide to do something crazy. I'm going to ring Simon Beresford. Right away. Just like that. I'm going to find that business card he gave me, dial the number and pretend I need a reference or something. Ridiculous, I know. Obvious, I know. He'll think it's really weird that I'm ringing three months later. Well, he'll think it's weird that I'm ringing him. Full stop. He might even have to stop for a minute to recall who I am – if I manage to get through to him. The worst that can happen is he gives me a reference and then flicks me off, politely, in the way a Buddhist might gently tap away a fly. But I'm going to do it anyway. Embarrassing, yes, but not the most embarrassing thing that's happened in the history of the universe. It doesn't compare, say, to The Daily Mail taking the worst ever photo of you and posting it on Daily Mail Online. In terms of mistakes, it doesn't compare to Tony Blair getting into bed with George Bush Junior and bombing Iraq.

I tap in the numbers and wait while it rings. I prepare myself for it going onto voicemail – or perhaps even being intercepted by a secretary.

"Hello?"

"Oh… hello! It's just Beanie, Sabina Upsell, here. I temped for you about three months ago? I don't know if you remember me? I was just… um…"

"Sabina? Yes, of course… I haven't seen you on the train lately."

"Actually, I've moved."

"How exceptionally disappointing!"

"To the seaside. Just for a break, temporarily, kind of thing."

"Ah. So where exactly?"

"Quinton. I'm renting in Quinton-on-Sea for now."

"Quinton?"

"Yes… Quinton-on-Sea. So… I just signed up with a temping agency here. I thought I might need a reference."

"Well, of course. Would you like me to email you?"

"That would be great! So, my email is: s.upsell1@ ukzoom.net."

"O…kay… so… got it. I'll get that off for you, Sabina. No problem!"

"Thanks! That's brilliant! Thanks so much!"

"No problem… I have a Great Aunt in Quinton-on-Sea who I visit sometimes. Lovely place."

"You think so? Well, if you ever find yourself in

Quinton-on-Sea… well, you know… just if ever…"

"Shall I give you a buzz next time I'm down?"

"Well, sure!"

"I wouldn't mind popping down there very soon. But I'm off to America tomorrow – to Cape Cod for two weeks. My eldest daughter's getting married."

"You have a grown-up daughter? Wow. How lovely. I hope you have a lovely time."

"Well, I think it *will* be… apart from the ex being there. Ex number one, that is, as opposed to ex number two!"

"So… so maybe I'll see you some time when you're next visiting your Great Aunt?"

"Actually, how about this evening?"

17

The Candy Box

With meeting Simon tonight, and then temping next week, it increases my sense that I need to prepare my appearance and I end up drifting into town, into a department store, and into the makeup section. I hold my hand up to my nose to try and avoid inhaling the smell of the perfume counter and select a small glass bottle of foundation that has its own little dispensing pump. A girl wearing a clinical-looking white overall, the kind that a dentist might wear, approaches.

"Are you being looked after, madam? Have you been colour matched?"

"Do I need to be?"

"To match your skin tone. Take a seat. Would you like to try the colour match as part of a complimentary make-over, madam?"

"A make-over?"

Next thing, I'm sitting in the demonstration chair. Firstly she wipes my face with a cotton-wool ball dabbed with toner. Then with a small brush she covers every nook and cranny of my face and even my eyelids with the foundation, as though she's painting a wall and she mustn't miss even the tiniest bits. I think about remonstrating but the young, eager face darting back and forth towards my own seems so dedicated to what she's doing that I decide to succumb to the process. Afterwards, looking in the mirror, I have to admit I look more like someone who's made a conventional effort.

"Would madam like to treat herself to any of these products today?"

Having been the recipient of so much exertion, I spend £40 on foundation and mascara. Then I go back home and wash it all off.

Louis thinks it's a terrific idea that Simon is joining us at The Candy Box. He's driving down from Blackheath – it's only an hour's trip – and will meet us all there.

The lighting in the long, narrow bar is low and ambient. Above us, a starball sparkles and, along the facing wall, squares pulsate with ever-changing colours, like a disco floor. I read the posters around the bar area:

Poptastic Nights at the Candy Box
With Drag DJ Topsie Smith
Every Friday 8pm till late

Get Up, Stand Up
Comedy Night at the Candy Box
The First Wednesday of the Month
8pm

Waking the Dead
La Chambre Magique Proudly Presents:
Ambient Grooves and Breakbeats
The Marina, 9pm-5am, Saturday 29 August
Dance Till Dawn
The Vibe Will Never Die

The latter has a graphic of a human body, showing the circulatory system, which I find a bit unappealing. Walking the Dead? It sounds horrible. I've never quite understood electronic music and loud, thumping beats.

Louis, me, and his friends Juliet, Elsa and Richard, settle ourselves on a circle of red leather pouffes around a glass table – the kind of space where the down-from-Londoners probably sip espresso during the day. Louis is wearing a pristine white shirt that highlights his tan from Barcelona, making him look as brown and shiny as a conker. He explains to everyone that, "Beanie's waiting for a date" and instructs them to "act natural" when he arrives, which causes some laughter, some partially suppressed and some not suppressed at all.

I'm glad the bar is quite dark, and I'm praying everyone will be a bit drunk by the time he arrives. I'm hoping everything gets a bit hazy, that the sharp edges of reality and people's observation faculties become a bit blurred – as quickly as possible, because he could arrive any moment now.

I feel pleasantly hazy by the time the first drink kicks-in – relaxed, hypnotised by the dark of the bar, with just the sparkles and the pulses.

"Who's going to *Waking the Dead* tomorrow?" asks Louis.

"*Waking* the Dead? I thought it said *Walking the Dead*."

"Walking the Dead? What are you like? You can go to a zombie convention if you want to, but I'm going to a rave, Beanie dearest."

Elsa, Juliet and Richard are laughing.

"It's fun having Beanie here. You should bring her along more often!" says Juliet.

I suddenly realise I've made a terrible mistake in meeting Simon here, surrounded by all of Louis's friends. I long for us to be meeting alone. I'm just thinking this when the door opens. He's here and walking towards us. He's still in his work clothes – a summer, linen suit, teamed with a floral retro-design tie.

Someone wolf-whistles.

"Is that *him*?" asks Elsa.

"Wow, he looks quite gay," says Louis in a lowered voice, "He must be *at least* bi."

"*Nice* tie!" says Juliet.

I stand up, engulfed by the sense of a mini-universe exploding into being, mixed with my self-consciousness.

"So this is where you've been hiding, Sabina! I kept looking out for you on the train, you know." He looks down at me, smiling. Overcome, I glance down at the table, at the lights pulsating on the floor. I'm glad the lighting is low.

"I was really worried that you were still ill."

"No, I've been fine, thanks! Really well."

"Let me get you a drink. Let me get a round. What would everyone like?"

"No, worries, Simon!" chirps Louis, "I've just ordered a pitcher of mojitos for everyone… Do you like mojito? Let me get you a glass. Or would that be a Sex On The Beach for you, Beanie?"

"No, I'll have a mojito, thank you very much."

Simon looks startled. "Your friend's quite outspoken, isn't he?"

"He is," I say.

He sits down next to me on a rectangular ottoman, beside the low table around which we're gathered. Luckily, the music – the pop-tastic music now being played by Drag DJ Topsie Smith – gets louder, enough to give us privacy from the others.

"I was really glad when you called."

"I'm glad that you're glad!" I say. "It's really nice that you're here."

"That's good. I'm glad I'm here, too."

"I like your cologne. Is it sandalwood?"

"Cedarwood."

"I was wondering what it was. Ever since the day on the train."

"It's a natural perfume; it's supposed to be very calming. It feels quite effective when you put the essential oil *here*."

As he says "here", he touches my temple. His fingertips rest for a moment, as light as a butterfly.

We sip our mojitos and the music gets even louder, so we give up trying to talk. People start dancing. I seemed to have downed my mojito within a few minutes and

Simon gets up, insists on buying another round. The bar area is quite narrow. I observe a good-looking guy pass behind Simon, en route back from the loos.

"Oh, sorry darling," he says, squeezing past. He puts his hands either side of Simon's waist as he passes. Louis seems quite drunk and invites Simon to sit next to him; he seems to be introducing all his gay female friends to me, as if to compensate.

After a couple more rounds of drinks, we all head to Uncle Tom's Cabin to see My Favourite Biscuit. There is a slightly raucous atmosphere and Simon puts his arm protectively around me. Later he holds my hand. It feels cool. Clinical and cool, bypassing all the historical debris inside me.

A girl in tight white jeans and high heels enters the bar and immediately strikes a pose, her chest out and her right arm stretched up towards the ceiling.

"My Favourite Biscuit!" she shouts. She pretends to pole dance around one of the pillars near the stage and shouts out, turning to each band member, "Have I shagged you? I can't remember… I know I've shagged you, yes, you, definitely…" She begins gyrating to the music with wild abandon.

What will Simon think? Immaculate Simon, with his soft Italian shirt and rich European look. Simon is stone-cold sober (apart from one mojito) because he's driving. What will he think? He looks startled.

"I've never been anywhere like this! It's quite good fun!" he says. But he has to go. He has to check in at the airport tomorrow at 7am.

I look around for Louis, but he's not there. I ask Juliet, "Where's Louis?"

"He's got a sugar craving. He's gone back to The Candy Box."

Simon offers to drive me back to my flat in his little MG roadster. Outside the front door, he stands close to me. In the dark, I can feel myself smiling; I can feel the smile on his face, too. I want him to kiss me with a certainty – a certainty; a feeling that I've waited for all my life. I feel a slight hesitation, though, about him seeing my strange seafront flat, with the furniture looking like dolls-house furniture in the vast rooms, the clanking boiler, and the gassy smells in the stairwell. But I find myself moving involuntarily, reaching for my key. I want Simon to come in.

"Can I come in?"

"Yes," I say.

Simon rests his hand on my back as I push open the door.

"Hey! Beanie!" I turn round. Louis's standing there, right next to us, looking completely wasted.

"Hey, sorry to interrupt you guys, but I'm locked out... Can't find my keys... Left my jacket somewhere, keys still in the pocket..."

"What rotten luck!" Simon empathises.

"I don't suppose I could possibly crash in your sitting-room? You can just ignore me, I'll be out cold, overdone it, got to admit... did try the night-bell at The Marina... couldn't believe it – no answer. What's the point in the night-bell?... no answer. Rung all my friends. No one's answering. Light-weights. All gone to bed. Yeah, overdone it… don't worry, I'll be out cold, won't hear anything… But actually, *really* bad timing, I guess... I'll be fine… sort something out, no problem." He turns to go.

"Hey, Louis, it'll be fine! I'm not leaving you out on the street!"

"I've got a terribly early start tomorrow. I'd best head on back and you need to have a good sleep… it's rotten luck…happens to the best of us!" Then he leans down and whispers in my ear, "I'd love to see you when I get back."

"Are you sure? Even though my life is a bit… unsorted?"

He presses his lips against mine and draws me close again, stroking my hair. "We can sort everything out together." And then he's gone and the MG is driving away.

18

Stone Pineapple

I wake up very late. I've slept right through the clanking boiler sound that comes from upstairs. Even though it's 11am, I want to close my eyes again, but I realise Simon will have woken up hours ago; he's already on the plane to the U.S.

In some kind of belated attempt at synchronisation of body-clocks and time schedules, I decide to get up. I switch on my computer and Google images of Cape Cod. It sounds – and looks – quite glamorous. Without intending to at all, suddenly I find I'm imagining that I'm on the plane with him, en route to America. We're staying in a glamorous, architect-designed house near the beach. We take walks along the coast and I'm introduced to all his relatives, in the run-up to his daughter's wedding.

His ex-wife will be there. Even if he doesn't particularly like her any more, it puts the dampers on my drifty, pleasant thoughts. But then I work it into the scenario

– the ex-wife is there with her new husband and this means that Simon is even *more* glad that I'm there. I can feel his arm around my waist even more tightly as the introductions are made: "Elizabeth [or whatever her name is], meet Sabina…" The ex-wife gives me a scrutinising look, but his daughter is thrilled that her Dad is happy to have met someone he likes.

To make the fantasy more realistic, more logical, I start assessing the little adaptations I would need to make if Simon ever invited me away on a trip. I go through my wardrobe and wonder whether I should buy some new clothes. It's embarrassing to catch myself thinking like this, but it's just being realistic that you can't wear jeans, T-shirts, jumpers and work clothes, to every event in life. The Beanie Life that involved: home – train – work – train – back home, was one thing, but a life that would involve going out is another. The clothes that I've bought from charity shops for twenty years have served me very well… up until now, that is. I'm proud that my weekend sweatshirts are ragged at the sleeves. But maybe I've done my abstemious bit for the planet (and my bank balance) over the last 20 years; and now I should Google some new, organic cotton clothes?

Another even more embarrassing thought is that I don't cook. These three weeks that Simon is away – I mean, if it works out – could be my chance to practise cooking. I know it's ridiculous thinking ahead, which is why I won't even mention it to Louis, it's so embarrassing – like I'm thinking myself into the role of being Simon's wife or something. But it doesn't have to be anybody else's business if I want to practise baking a cake. In fact, I think I *will* practise baking a cake – today. Nobody needs to know. And I should practise a few gourmet vegetarian recipes, that kind of thing. I wonder if Simon is mostly vegetarian, too?

I'd quite like Louis to be out of the flat before I practise baking, because it's just my own little private thing. I'll make him an espresso and prise him gently out of bed. Although it's quite sunny outside... maybe I should go for a walk and let Louis sleep in? I head to the kitchen and find a note on the worktop – and realise that my dilemma about prising Louis out of bed has been overtaken by events:

Hey! This flat is a bit weird – ask yours truly for some advice next time! Simon, on the other hand, is quite a find. I felt quite envious when he was stroking your hair. Maybe there should be a phrase for it after all. Cinnamon Sex! Come round later for a cappuccino and a post mortem.

Thanks for helping me out of a tight spot last night. I hope I didn't interrupt anything – but anticipation is half the equation, so…. Anyway, all is well. DJ Topsie Smith rang to say my jacket (with keys safely stowed in pocket) has been found at The Candy Box.

Didn't want to disturb you. You need some beauty sleep before Waking the Dead?

See you later

Louis XX

I text Louis:

Gr8 that your keys r safe. Just having a slow start. Call u l8r X.

The sun is calling me outside, so I postpone my baking plan, pack my swimming costume and a towel and go for a slow walk along the seafront, savouring the hazy feeling from yesterday. The light has turned a little more golden, the way it does sometimes in the run-up to an Indian summer. I lie on the warm, pebbly beach, listening to the surf and close my eyes. The beach is a little busy to get totally into some fantasy about dark rooms. Besides which, I prefer to think about Simon's face, and imagine he's lying next to me on the beach in Cape Cod. In any event, it would be nice (a) to be with him and (b) to be living somewhere other than my gassy flat.

The water feels freezing as I wade in, but once I'm bobbing up and down in the waves, warm currents alternate with the icy ones. Miniature wavelets, right up to the horizon, sparkle in the light. I turn around and face the shore. Up on the cliff tops, I can see a line of giant trees, like a windbreak. The trees look strange because the lower canopies have green leaves, but the crowns are denuded of foliage. The upper branches reach skywards, bare, like skeletal arms. There's a small gap in the windbreak through which I can see a gleam, like sunlight reflected on a glass window, and a grey tower with a carved stone pineapple on top. Just at the top, right-hand side of the tower is another gleam, protruding, as though from an oriel window, and the purple blooms of a climbing tree – perhaps a wisteria – cascading around it.

I let the sea carry me until I'm quite far out, and then gradually swim back inland.

Back at the flat, I get out an old Delia Smith cookery book that my mother gave me about sixteen years ago, when I set off to work in London. I decide to make a sponge cake – but my own version of it, with less sugar. I flick through the index. Not a single cake recipe. Never mind, I'll Google a recipe! Something bang-up-to-the-minute, something from Pinterest, maybe!

I plump for a lemon and coconut cream 'cheesecake'. It's entirely vegan and even has drops of essential oil in the topping. What I need to be is *myself*, to cook but be *myself*, to make the kind of recipes that reflect who I really am – vegan (mostly), organic recipes, with the wow factor. Even Beyoncé and Jay-Z eat a plant-based diet, apparently. I don't need to worry about being a traditional hostess who can cook lamb casseroles, coq au vin, and all that old-fashioned stuff. So passé!

I'm going to need: ground almonds, coconut oil, lemon essential oil, walnuts, cashews, maple syrup and blueberries. It's going to be quite an expensive experiment. But it's true what Louis said – I don't let enough new things into my life. I've spent my life going round in circles in my small, comfort zone. It's time to break out.

Miraculously, I manage to track down all the ingredients as the local health food shop is pretty well stocked.

The cost has come to over £20, but that's okay as there will be ingredients left over for the next one. The base is crushed walnuts mixed with walnut oil. The topping is soaked, blended cashews mixed with ground almonds and… coconut oil. I'm slightly concerned that there's quite a lot of nut oil going on in this recipe – almost wholly, really, apart from the drops of essential oil, a few drops of maple syrup and the blueberries. But I press on, as the person who's posted the recipe says that she can't stop eating it, and she looks amazingly slim and healthy.

One hour later, I leave it to set in the fridge. I nibble the leftover bits of topping. It tastes a little bit like perfumed coconut oil melting in my mouth. It's quite a big 'cheesecake'. I wonder how I'm going to get through all that oil on my own.

The phone rings. If it's Simon, act casual. Don't mention the 'cheesecake'! Then I realise it can't be Simon; he's still up in the air somewhere.

"Hi Beanie. Are you coming to Waking the Dead tonight? Or perhaps you've already been woken from the dead after carousing on the town with Simon last night? I'm really, really sorry I interrupted…"

"Look, no worries. It wasn't my idea of the ideal venue for…"

"Yeah, it smells of gas, no kidding. I was lying in bed thinking there was going to be some kind of explosion and I'd wake up covered in rubble. Actually I think I did you a favour because you don't want the memory of your first shag to be infiltrated with the smell of some kind of gas leak."

"Anyway, I'm glad you got your jacket and your keys."

"Yeah, phew! Topsie Smith didn't seem to mind. I

think he's always wanted to rifle through my pockets. So you're not coming to Waking the Dead, Walking the Dead, Chambre Magique... I can't tempt you with any variation?"

I recall the strange picture of the human body and its circulatory system and the zany, bulbous lettering, with electric-blue and red lines around it, on the poster. I prefer the idea of staying in. I've bought a bottle of cedarwood essential oil from the health food shop, so I can smell it and be reminded of Simon. Perhaps he'll be ringing later. I'd like to put on some nice music, scatter my pillow with drops of cedarwood oil, then lie in bed and think about Simon.

"I don't think I'll make it. Sorry to be a party pooper."

"There's a whole bunch of us meeting round at my place first for a bite to eat. At least come for the meal."

"I'm so tired, Louis. I hope you don't mind if I just stay in. It's all been go-go-go. But I don't suppose you'd like a freshly made vegan cheesecake to dole out to your friends? It's quite... oily? I think it's going to need a lot of people in order to get rid of it. I don't suppose I could drop it off at your place?"

"Charming. Okay, bring it round. Why on earth did you suddenly make a big, oily cheesecake, anyway?"

19

Chambre Magique

I lie awake, looking at the full moon through the gap in my curtains. I can never sleep when it's a full moon. *Boys and girls come out to play, the moon doth shine as bright as day.* And then I remember: *waking the dead... waking the dead.* I get up and go through the items in my wardrobe. I'm not going to actually go to the rave, I just want to see if I've got anything to wear. I put on some jeans, a black halter-neck top, a small chocolate-brown suede jacket, some low-heeled strappy shoes that I used to wear for work. I spray on my frankincense organic perfume and look in the mirror. Despite my low self-esteem, I think I look quite good. The Marina. Where is the Marina? Marine... the sea... I head to the seafront and keep going, towards the sound of the thudding bass. Suddenly, it feels like some primitive call.

Outside the Marina, on the beach, a girl in a green jumpsuit is twirling weighted cords with lighted wicks on each end. Rhythmically, she swings the cords around her body, creating circles of fire, then figures of eight, in the dark. I find the entrance to the Bauhaus-style building and go in. Inside, it's a wonderland: laser-lights, strobe lights, jungle rhythms, people of all ages – plenty of aging, grey-haired old punks, as well as young people. I can't see Louis anywhere. I head into a room with sofas called the 'Ambient Lounge' and sit in a deep, low chair, sipping my complimentary Sambuca. A girl next to me with a butterfly tattoo on her arm asks if I, "would like a sweetie" and opens her clasped hand to reveal a small pill with a smiley face.

"What if I die?" I ask.

The girl laughs and I laugh as I wash the pill down with a sip of Sambuca. I couldn't do this if Simon were here. Maybe it's good to have this kind of experience before he gets back, because if things work out, I'm ready to do the conventional thing. But I should have this experience first.

I sit deep in the armchair for a long time, just watching, wondering if I feel any different. I'm not sure. But when I eventually get up to dance, something is different. The girl with the butterfly tattoo smiles at me and I smile back, a conspiratorial smile. Above the beat is a woman's voice: *This is my house. Welcome to my house. In my house everyone is free to be who they really are.* I feel powerful. It feels as though the universe is whispering secrets to me, conquering other voices, voices from the past. My stepfather's voice: *This is my house, and in my house you'll do as I say.* Frightening voices, now as silly as a puff of smoke, as the woman says once again: *Welcome to my house…*

The Marina is underneath the promenade, at sea level. It feels underground. I feel I understand what 'underground' means as I dance. It's something that the banks and all the corporate systems can never quite control, they will never be able to master it. Images of cityscapes are projected onto a wall – New York, London, Tokyo. It's all just background, when you can feel who you really are. I don't actually care if I'm feeling this because I've taken a pill, I don't care at all. The girl with the butterfly tattoo on her arm smiles at me over her shoulder, in our shared secret, as she glides past. I can hear different layers in the music. I concentrate on the deep bass, but somehow my body moves to a syncopated beat as well.

I'm still dancing when I see there's a slight sense of commotion near the entrance – just the commotion of a few late arrivals. I'm aware of a shock of steel-grey and white hair that's parted at the side, a tall frame that's dressed in electric-blue jeans, a deep purple shirt and a black jacket. To say the expression on his face was a sneer would be too strong; but it's an expression that has no need to answer to anyone, an expression that's as fully present in the aged face, as unapologetic as any young Gucci model in his prime. By the door, he picks up a glass of complimentary Sambuca, throws his head back and downs the shot in one. The girl behind the table offers him another one, they exchange words, and now he's smiling – an engaging, sociable, exquisite smile. He downs the second shot. There is an entourage of gilded youth around him, both male and female. People are greeting him as he walks to the bar. The young entourage follow in his wake. It looks like a rock star just made an entrance. It's *him*. It's Ossian Brohmer.

2 0

Ossian

I carry on dancing. Although it's exciting that Ossian Brohmer is here, I don't feel any need to do anything, like rush over to the bar. The music has me in its sway. It doesn't feel like an artificial experience. I know now how I'm meant to feel. This was the purpose of life all along, to feel like this, not to have to 'get through it'. This is who I really am. I close my eyes as I dance. I see the music in colours. Now the voice above the beat is saying, "This is only a test. This is only a test." And I know what the voice means. We're here as some kind of experiment. Don't get bogged down in it. It's only a test.

Eventually, I head to the bar. I still can't see Louis or 'his tribe' anywhere. Normally, I'd feel paranoid about being on my own, but, with this feeling of being in touch with myself, it doesn't seem to matter at all. I'm waiting at the bar when I hear a voice right behind me.

"I was watching *you* dance."

I turn around. It's Ossian Brohmer, surrounded

still by the group of gilded youth. He has neither the engaging smile on his face, nor the diffident, near-sneer. He looks neutral, like he's making a detached statement of fact. The faces of the young people look towards me eagerly, smiling, rather than dismayed that their maestro is momentarily distracted by someone outside the group. Ossian Brohmer is looking at *me*. I exist in his eyes now. The face I first looked at twenty years ago is looking at *me*. I stay calm, despite the fact that the image of me, Beanie Upsell, is being projected onto Ossian Brohmer's retinas, is being absorbed into the mind that conjured *The Index of Dreams*.

"You're a very good dancer."

"Thank you."

I'm close enough to see the slight perspiration on his face.

"There's something interesting about you… sorry, what's your name?"

"Beanie."

"Beanie? I'm Ossian." He extends a hand.

"I know," I say, as I slide my hand into his. His handshake is brief, firm.

The universe is playing some kind of trick on me. A beautiful trick. A beautiful illusion.

"You know that you're interesting or you know that my name is Ossian?"

The gilded youth laugh – in a pleasant way.

"I know that you're Ossian Brohmer. I don't want to bore you, but I waited 20 years to see *The Index of Dreams*."

"It doesn't bore *me*. I just hope it didn't bore *you*, after waiting all that time."

"Oh no! Not at all! I think it's the best film I've ever seen!"

"Is it, now? Well, I'm always pleased to meet a satisfied customer."

The young girl who is foremost, standing at his side, smiles at me enthusiastically. She looks immaculate, as though she brushed her shiny, long brown hair and did her make-up five minutes ago. And she's *young*; maybe twenty years old.

"This is my PA, Lola." The twenty-year-old smiles again at me. "And this is her friend, Pixie, who's in my latest film."

Pixie moves her petite body in time to the music, just an imperceptible movement, as though there's no rush to dance, as though she has opportunities to dance all the time. Her halter-neck dress is long, her neck and arms adorned with beads and gems. She whispers in Lola's ear and then kisses her cheek.

The person at the bar wants to take Ossian's order.

"I'll have three gin and tonics and... what are you having, Beanie?"

"Just water."

"...And just water. That's very abstemious of you, Beanie. There again, it *is* nearly dawn."

I thank Ossian for the water and as I turn to head back to the dance floor, he says, in his neutral tone, "Maybe you *should* know that you look rather interesting."

I carry on dancing. I can see him in the distance, heading towards the exit, with Lola and Pixie in tow, holding their gin and tonics, walking behind him in their flip-flops with measured paces, as though joined by some invisible rope, still with smiling, non-possessive expressions on their faces. I close my eyes and keep dancing; smiling. Chambre Magique. I bask in magic.

The music stops. I look at my watch. It's 5am. The lights go off for a split second and then on again, to indicate that it's the end. It's finished too soon. Normally, I'm keen on endings, glad that things are over, happy to go to bed and shut my eyes, relieved of the need to make any effort for a while – and, if I'm lucky, experience the oblivion of deep sleep. But not now. I want this to go on and on.

Outside, it's still dark. The remains of the throng have gathered in a lingering post-party mood. Suddenly I see Louis and his 'tribe' sitting on the pebbly beach, around a fire made of driftwood. I'm about to head towards the railings, to get onto the beach, when I find Ossian standing in front of me, together with his coterie. He inhales on a joint and then flips it round and jabs it in front of me.

"Oh, thank you," I say. I put the joint to my lips, the joint that has just been in Ossian Brohmer's lips, and inhale.

The relative novelty of the smoke on my throat causes me to splutter.

"Oops. I haven't smoked for a while."

"Well, don't let me *force* you into anything," says Ossian. The girls titter. "Anyway, so we're just heading back to mine for some breakfast. I was wondering if you'd care to join us?"

"Oh, thank you. That sounds really nice." I take a mini-puff of the joint this time, which I don't really inhale, before passing it on to Pixie. "Have I got time just to run over to my friend Louis, to say 'hi'? I was looking out for him all night."

"Sure. You go and see Louis."

I run across the pebbles.

"You're here!" says Louis. "You little raver! Have you been here all night?"

"Yes! I've taken an E!"

"What, your first ever E?"

"Yes!"

"What were you *doing* in the 1990s? Oh, I forget, you were still a child back then. But still, what were you *doing* in the late 90s and all through the noughties? Not being naughty enough, obviously. All I can say is you're lucky there were some half decent pills going around tonight. Normally they're rubbish, these days."

"But where were you? I was looking for you!"

"Tripping the light fantastic, down here on the beach, darling."

"I've got to go. I'm having breakfast with Ossian Brohmer."

Juliet stifles a giggle.

"Are you actually going to Ossian's *house*?" asks Louis.

"Yes!"

"What about Simon?"

"What *about* Simon? I'm only going for *breakfast*."

"Breakfast, hey?" says Elsa.

"Yes, me, Pixie, Lola and Ossian. Please don't be mean about this, Louis. I'm having *such* a nice time."

"Enjoy it," says Juliet, "It's not like he'll force you into anything. He just tries to overpower with his charm. Remember, you're just the next piece of candy. He's like a busy bee, likes to try a little sip from each new flower."

"He's not taking any sip from me! I'm very, very keen on Simon."

"Just be particularly wary if he asks if you've ever thought about being an actress. That's when you should see a red light flashing!"

"I've got to go. I'll ring you later, Louis!"

For a moment, I can't see Ossian. I wonder if I've spent too long talking to Louis and the others on the beach, and I've missed my chance – missed my chance for a trip to the house up on the cliffs, the chance for a tête-à-tête with Ossian Brohmer, to become his friend, to become his cleaner, perhaps. To be the person who could understand him! And to be there with the other girls, who are very sweet; whose presence is necessary, in fact, to make the whole thing light, breezy and innocent.

I see a police car pull up on the sea front and two uniformed police officers get out. They head towards the Marina entrance. Then I hear a suave, disdainful voice, a voice that is now familiar, behind me.

"Oh my God, the pigs are here! I thought I could smell a terrible smell!" It's Ossian. He's here again, with Pixie and Lola in tow. "I think it's time to make a move!" he says, raising his arms and encompassing all of us, like a mother hen gathering her brood.

2 1

The Medicine Chest

I've just woken up in Ossian Brohmer's bed. He's asleep still, with his clothed back to me. I'm not sure how I got here. I don't mean I *literally* don't know how I got here. It's not that he slipped rohypnol into my drink and I blacked out. I remember what happened. And nothing *major* has happened.

I simply followed Ossian, with Pixie and Lola, as though I had joined them on the 'invisible rope' behind the maestro, down to the old town and then up some carved steps in the cliff-face.

"Welcome to my folly!" announced Ossian, breathlessly, as we climbed the last of the steps, and headed towards the gap in the line of trees – towards the very same tower that I had seen peeping through the wall of trees whilst swimming yesterday. I could see now that it had a small cottage attached on the left-hand side.

Just for a moment, I turned and looked back. The sun was just beginning to brim over the horizon with a shimmering hint of orange. It felt like a powerful place to be, looking down on all the dwellings below and the hubbub of the town – something that you could participate in, but escape from, too. The houses below looked small, like sweets packed in a box, and the funfair looked no bigger than a toy. Up here was a vantage point, a place where you could believe anything was possible – although, on turning back round, I felt struck by the strange atmosphere of the place.

"Is there something wrong with these trees?" I asked.

"I don't know," said Ossian. "All I know is they're beginning to look a bit decrepit, like everything else around here."

"Is it ash dieback? I saw a feature on the news…"

Ossian was now ahead, his back to me. Lola put a warning finger to her lips and whispered, "Best not to mention it. The Council have been hassling him about it."

Ossian turned slightly, as though aware of the whispering. I caught sight of his face in profile, with his eyes lowered and his mouth grim, downturned, dejected.

Although the brimming orange on the horizon promised another hot summer's day, the line of ash cast a chilly darkness over the building. The sea winds of past wintry storms – or, perhaps, just the effects of time – had ravaged the lichen-covered stone pineapple, and a few of its carved leaves lay strewn on the unkempt grass, along with pieces of yellow stucco that had peeled away from the tower.

"The Victorians used to grow pineapples and exotic fruits in this thing – heated by trenches of steamy manure! But don't worry, the only thing growing inside now is the odd patch of mould! The cottage was for the gardener. The main house..." Ossian pointed to a jungle of rosebay willowherb and the occasional fallen obelisk, in the distance, "...was destroyed by a fire in the 1950s."

We followed him round to the back of the cottage, where he put a key in the Gothic-shaped wooden door. Inside, standing in the stone-flagged hallway, I could, in fact, smell quite severe damp or mould. A pile of unopened post lay scattered to one side, as though it was some kind of unoccupied rental property.

In the kitchen, the vestiges of the previous occupier's taste lay in evidence, untouched: the marble-effect lino, formica kitchen units circa 1970, an Artexed ceiling, and orange and brown flowery tiles.

"Welcome to the vintage kitchen! Sit yourselves down!"

The only evidence I could see of Ossian's ownership were the holiday snaps, girlfriend photos, and postcards pinned to a cork board. My eyes glutted on the images: Ossian standing next to what looked like a private plane with a tall girl, as pretty as a model, their hair swept up in the wind, blowing across sun-burnished faces, and, behind them, blue, blue sky. A young, Scandinavian-looking woman in a wicker chair, in the Lotus position, gazing at the camera with a spontaneous smile. On the patio around her, kumquat trees sat in giant terracotta pots and, in the foreground, a pomegranate hung from a branch. There was Ossian with the model again, this time at what looked like a masquerade ball, in a night-time garden lit with flares and fairy lights; the rolling lawn and huge house in the distance spoke of Palladian mansions and Capability Brown landscapes.

I settled myself on a velveteen cushion in the window-seat, while Pixie and Lola sat at the table, and Ossian went to work with the frying pan. I sipped the delicious espresso that he made, and came to the conclusion that Ossian was a true bohemian. Unlike my parents, who agonised over every small fitting and door handle, Ossian just didn't seem to care – as though who he was, and how he was judged, had nothing to do with his surroundings.

Not that I aspired to live in quite such a dilapidated place. But I felt my imagination running ahead of me: how I would clean it up for Ossian so he could sell it and move to somewhere full of light and reclaimed – but smooth and shiny – timber. Somewhere that spoke of Nordic beauty.

It was after we had eaten – eggs fried to smithereens and fried bread – that Ossian suggested a morning swim. In his bedroom – a small dark chamber, with a crimson carpet and heavy oak furniture – he opened a drawer containing clothes that had been left behind by previous girlfriends, and I had a selection of about five bikinis to choose from. He handed out towels and then it was back down the carved steps, down to the beach, which we had to ourselves.

Once we had left the house, it felt like riding the crest of a wave, with one pleasure unrolling after the next. When I was small I always felt I got punished if I'd had a nice time, a nice day out, as if to bring me back to harsh reality. But in this new wonderland, life unfurled, like petals on a flower.

We splashed into the high tide, the pebbles shelved away beneath us, and the large waves lifted us off our feet and bobbed our bodies up and down, like sailboats on a choppy sea. It seemed, then, that it wasn't about dualities, this choice or that choice, but about enjoying life, enjoying every relationship, male or female; being free to enjoy each man's company, because not every exchange with another person had to mean physical consummation.

It was while we were bobbing in the waves that Ossian said, "You're like somebody who's between two worlds. I imagine you're quite hard to pin down."

"Maybe because I'm dysfunctional. I'd rather *not* be hard to pin down."

"You're someone who's not easily impressed, that's the truth of it. Someone bullied you into thinking you must always be polite, especially to men. But underneath, you're not easily impressed."

"I hadn't thought of it like that. I'm quite insecure."

"Yes, when you are finally impressed, you're insecure."

"You seem to know a lot about me, even though you've only just met me."

"I wonder what you'd look like on film."

"I don't know. I've never seen myself on film."

"Never?" said Ossian. "I'm on location tomorrow. Just for rehearsals and test shots. Why don't you come along?"

It felt like another unfurling of rose petals. It didn't feel like a red light flashing. Yes, it felt like a light – the light into which Beanie Upsell was walking, leaving the darkness and obscurity and ignominy of her life behind.

Then I remembered I was supposed to start at the police station tomorrow. Would I dare lie to the police? We were carried up and down in the rise and fall of another undulation. The waves slapped and sparkled around me.

"Sure! That sounds like fun!" I said.

Back on the beach, he tapped my contact details into his phone.

"I'll pick you up from outside The Marina tomorrow morning. I'll be in my groovy racing green Morris Minor. Let's say 6am?"

Then we lay on our beach towels for a while, absorbing the hot rays of the sun. The image of the Sun Card in the Tarot came to mind with its full beams, the unfurled sunflowers, the little child on the white horse and the sense of abundance, energy, adventure.

"Talking of film scripts… can I ask you a question?"

"Fire away!"

"Do you ever feel just brimming with energy to make lots of films? Do you have moments where everything seems *so* full of possibility? Where ideas just tumble from the unconscious? I just wondered… once you have all the equipment and you *know* how to make a film… it's like magic, isn't it? Creating these scenes, these dramas? How you can make a life by *playing*!"

"You have such a sweet enthusiasm, Beanie. I'm afraid you're talking to a somewhat frazzled old bean. Taken a few knocks in life. Had the stuffing knocked out of me a bit. So you see, Beanie, I'm afraid it's not *quite* so simple as that."

"You know in *The Index of Dreams*… it's all very beautiful. I was wondering… in terms of it being realistic and everything… did you ever consider including characters who want to die because they're addicted to something… I mean, did you ever think about making *The Index* more realistic by incorporating more *extreme* cases like addicts and alcoholics who might want to die?"

I lay on my side, propping up my head with one

hand and marvelled how I was talking to the Director himself; here I was in a one-on-one scenario with Ossian Brohmer, able to hear the answer directly from the horse's mouth.

His profile faced upwards, towards the sun, his eyes closed. I reflected on how his choice of swimwear was tasteful – a pair of classic navy shorts: not loose and baggy like a surfer, nor eye-wateringly clingy. Not clingy at all. Just trim. The kind of swimming trunks that, if someone had asked me what kind my ideal man would wear... well, they'd be just like this. It made me wonder how much a woman is drawn or repelled by a man's choice of clothing and how Ossian's electric blue jeans and purple shirt also drew me to him. Made me feel I could be around him. Be around him always – because there's nothing stuffy about a man who wears electric blue and deep purple. Nor ever likely to be... stuffy, dull, making me feel trapped.

The muscles in Ossian's forehead twitched and a deep furrow appeared between his eyes.

"Lucky, you've caught me in a relaxed mood, Beanie. One thing I'm not looking forward to when *The Index* is uncensored is that people start asking all these questions. Ridiculous questions..."

"Sorry..."

"Irrelevant questions. I mean, what do *you* think?"

"I'm not sure, actually..."

Ossian rolled onto his side, facing me.

"Can you imagine all these people turning up at *The Index of Dreams* shouting for a fix? The heroin addicts scratching themselves, chucking their used syringes under the hedges?"

"No, not really."

"Exactly. It's supposed to be a film about beauty. The beauty of the death wish. Not about some half-addled people turning up there like zombies. It's about tuning into feelings. I mean, if a heroin addict wants to end it all, they've got the means to do it any time. A girl like Stina, she didn't have that choice. She didn't want to go down a slippery slope before death. To grub around with dealers. To lose control. She wanted to be herself. You remember the scene where Stina and the others share how they can feel something's gone wrong in their DNA, not their literal DNA, but in their programming?"

"Mm hm."

"They can feel it in their bones. They sense that they can never get back on track. Like a tree that's going to grow in the wrong direction – out to the side, instead of straight up. Or like a tree that's diseased. They're just acorns, these young people. They want to end it all while they're still acorns, still seedlings, before their beauty's totally snuffed out, because they sense that things aren't going to turn out well. They want to die in their prime, not get through years of struggle, and then die ravaged, perhaps as an addict. You disappoint me, Beanie…"

There was something about being really tired that made me tearful. It happens whenever I've stayed up all night. I tried desperately hard to hold the emotion down; it throbbed, painfully, in my throat. In the distance, I could see Pixie and Lola still bobbing carefree in the waves, buoyant, laughing.

"Sorry…"

"Hey!" Ossian gently placed a finger on my cheek where salty tears ran down, mixing with the sun-dried seawater on my lips. "I didn't mean to upset you. It's just you're the sort of person I wanted the film for. I didn't want it to be some bloody gritty social drama, full of urban realism. I wanted it to be for the Beanies of this world. Sweet, young people full of Keatsian poetry, 'straining at particles of light in the midst of a great darkness.'"

We basked a while longer in the mid-morning sun, and then Ossian suggested lunch as he had some home-made bouillabaisse in the fridge.

"What's bouillabaisse?" I asked.

"It's a classic French seafood soup. We have ze lobster, ze clams, ze shrimps, ze white fish, ze saffron, ze bay leaves and ze pommes de terre," said Ossian in a mock French accent.

There goes my no seafood rule, my self-imposed rule due to decimation of sea-stocks and the sea-bed, I thought. It sounded delicious. In fact, I probably needed some of the minerals and Omega 3s in it. Like a neces-sary dose.

"Don't worry. I didn't boil the lobster alive. I dispatched it with one swift stab of the knife."

"That's reassuring," I said.

It was after the delicious bouillabaisse lunch, served with garlic bread and white wine, that Pixie said, "Let's crash," as though it were the most natural thing in the world, as though this was the plan all along. Lola and Pixie took the spare rooms and Ossian invited me to share 'the other side' of his vast expanse of a bed, in the room with the crimson carpet. "No touching!" he joked.

Even though he'd said, "No touching" in a jokey way, I stood in the bathroom wondering whether his intentions *were* anything beyond sleep. I had been warned: Louis, Juliet... I cupped my hand around my nose and mouth and breathed on it, testing my breath. Did it smell of the fishy bouillabaisse? I caught sight of myself in the mirror and, as though caught in some act of preparation, felt silly. Was it true he had a girlfriend up in London? Nevertheless, I picked up a tube of toothpaste and squirted a mini slug onto my finger and rubbed it around my teeth.

I looked at my face in the mirror, wondering whether it was just a coincidence or whether the universe had answered my prayer – whether, very slowly, over the course of twenty years, various sub-atomic particles of my thought pattern had gone out into the world and somehow caused this meeting to happen. And how, in a sense, I had no choice but to go forwards into this encounter. I felt guilty because it was as though something vital that was lost and buried for twenty years was starting to beat again, it was going to override everything else. It was going to override Simon – although I didn't know what form it would take, this collision of particles between Ossian and myself.

I rinsed and went through to the bedroom. Ossian's had his back towards me and, from the regular sound of the inhalation and exhalation, I could tell he was already asleep. Ossian Brohmer – love rat, Casanova, cad – was dead to the world. I wasn't sure whether I felt rejected or let off the hook.

There was one moment, somewhere in-between waking and sleep, when Ossian rolled over and wrapped his arms around me. It felt healing, forgiving. As though he forgave me for my question on the beach. As though it had brought us closer, somehow. In that moment, I felt the struggle of my whole life had been worth it for an experience such as this… to have the part of me that was buried, tired, safely embraced by Ossian Brohmer.

Ossian Brohmer, conjuror, Director of *The Index of Dreams*, with his demeanour of disdain that was both alluring and slightly frightening. The flash of tenderness appeared like a chink through his Nordic armour… perhaps it was this very fact that made it feel so special. Real. Authentic. Not like some sloppy, eager-to-please thing that was following a script, following expectations, rehearsed, copied from all that went before in the history of romantic literature.

So this is how it's possible to wake up in another man's bed within forty-eight hours of my date with Simon. It feels like someone has changed the disks of my life in quick succession. Yesterday, it was as if everything had been leading up to meeting Simon. But then someone pressed 'Stop', 'Eject', and inserted a different film – a film that had lain in waiting for twenty years; a film that was reclaiming my lost teenage self, surging into the present with a mythological force that, despite the chaste nature of my interlude in Ossian's bed, would overpower everything else. I feel like one of those animals in the Sahara desert that waits underground, for years, until the rain comes. And then it surfaces. The desert blooms. But it's more complicated than that for a human being. It's not just a desert blooming, but a fork trying to wedge itself into the road, changing the outlook, obscuring the singularity of my focus.

I look at my watch, trying to work out what time it is in Cape Cod. Do I need to listen out for a phone call or a text from Simon? It's now 4pm. That makes it about 11am in America. I don't have my phone here.

Suddenly, I want to get home to check for messages. Why has the universe sent this conflict? "It's only a test. This is only a test," I remind myself. But everything is happening too quickly. I want the horizon to be wide, open, untrammelled for my experience 'on location'.

I press my temples with my index fingers, trying to ease the slight throbbing of a headache, and then slip out of the bed, quietly – very quietly, so as to leave Ossian slumbering, as undisturbed as a kraken in the deep – and put my jeans back on. It hits me like a wave, not a small wave, but a huge breaker, right in my centre: I'm here, in Ossian Brohmer's house. Not just in his house, but his bedroom. That's Ossian Brohmer in the bed. Ossian Brohmer. How can it be that the life of Beanie Upsell, secretary, has intersected with the life of Ossian Brohmer, film director?

I'm drawn by the smell of fresh coffee into the kitchen, where Lola, dressed in a pair of white cut-offs and a crochet crop top, is sitting cross-legged on a chair, crouched over a sleek laptop.

"Good morning!"

"It's afternoon, actually, Beanie."

"Oh, sorry! Good afternoon! I don't suppose there are any painkillers knocking around are there?"

"Sure. Follow me."

I follow Lola back upstairs to the landing. In a recess, on a shelf, sits an antique wooden box, with lots of small drawers and compartments.

"It's a ship's medicine cabinet." Lola opens a drawer and takes out a packet of supermarket-branded pain-killers. "One or two?"

"Just one, please." She pops one out of the foil casing and into my hand.

Out of curiosity, I open another of the mini-drawers. There's a bottle of green, gelatine-encased capsules with a prescription label on the front. Feeling I've overstepped the mark, I quickly close the drawer.

"There's everything here." Lola opens and closes the drawers one by one. "Pills for waking up, pills for going to sleep, party drugs – cocaine, MDMA; and a couple of really naughty drugs, like heroin."

"Heroin?"

"He says he doesn't use it very often. Ossian says he uses drugs like changing gear. He likes to stay in control."

"That's good."

"But never take the pills in this one." Pixie taps a shell-pink fingernail on a small drawer with a lock on it.

"Why?"

"It's something from Mexico. Ossian refers to it as the ultimate exit strategy. That's all I know. He says it's all about control. About being able to control your life. Some people really disapprove. Actually, don't tell anybody what I've told you."

"Oh no, don't worry! I mean, I think all this is quite cool, actually. A mini-apothecary. Maybe everyone should have one."

I follow Lola back down to the kitchen and wash the tablet down with a delicious milky espresso, before setting off back down the carved steps to the beach and homewards.

I'm standing looking at the sea when everything that's happened hits me like a giant wave again. And he's invited me on set tomorrow. The excitement is edged with fear. Beanie Upsell is someone who, in the past, could barely handle the social interactions of office life and someone so non-expressive she was afraid to even sing 'Happy Birthday' to anyone. My only experience of being around drama is (i) being a shepherd in my primary school nativity and my mother gave me a hand-towel to put on my head as a scarf; and (ii) playing a servant in a school production of *Medea*.

But it's like the levee of holding back is full to the brim now. I have to go forwards. I don't want to cringe any more. I don't want to be mortified with embarrassment any more. The 15 years of crawling along in an office has cured me, has made me angry, even, perhaps. I'm only going to be on set, I'm not acting, but this is the real deal. It's not a school play. This is real life. I think back to my 14-year-old self. I feel the universe is inviting me back in time to what I wanted then, to somehow reach out and touch *The Index of Dreams*.

On the way home, I pass Louis's door. He's probably out on the beach, but I ring the buzzer anyway.

His voice comes through the intercom, a little groggy: "Hullo?"

"It's Beanie!"

The door release mechanism buzzes and I go in.

I lie on my side on Louis's couch while he's busy in the kitchen. I hear the pressurised steam as he heats the milk with his fancy espresso maker for our coffees. He comes through carrying a tray and places the perfect cappuccino, with a swirl pattern in the frothed milk, on the table in front of me.

"Have you got any Es?" I ask.

"What for?"

"No particular reason."

"Well, you don't need any on a Sunday afternoon, that's for sure, Beanie."

"I do, actually. I've been invited on location with Ossian tomorrow and, just as a one off, I'd like to feel, make sure I keep feeling, you know, more interesting."

"I'm not giving you a pill to take on a Monday morning. No way, Beanie. Anyway, I thought you were working at the police station tomorrow."

"I'm just going to postpone it for a day. It's a no brainer. I can't put a typing job in front of my chance to go on location with Ossian."

"Well, I don't keep a stash of them. So I'm not doling out any pills."

"Do you know anyone who does?"

"You mean a dealer? Christ, Beanie, what's got into you? I'll sort you out next time we're out for the evening, okay. That's it. So… you had a good time last night?"

"Amazing, actually. When's the next Chambre Magique? I want to go dancing again ASAP!"

"Clearly."

I gulp down my coffee and get up. "I'd better go. Busy day tomorrow."

I head towards the door but Louis bars my way. "Not so fast, sunshine! There's a bit of a post mortem to do. I want to know what happened at Ossian's."

"*Nothing* happened with Ossian. I just went to his house with Lola – who's his PA, actually – and her friend Pixie. We ate breakfast. We went to the beach. Swam. We had lunch. That's it. Okay, I admit his house does have a bit of a strange atmosphere and it probably needs at least thirty grand to sort it out. And perhaps a bit of a clean in the meantime."

"I bet he got you into his bed."

"Technically speaking, I slept for about three hours on one side of his emperor-size bed, with the space of about a metre between us. That's it!"

"I knew it. He's a tosser. Just don't sabotage what you've got with a decent guy for some womanising idiot. That's all!"

"Just because I've accepted Ossian's invite to go on location doesn't automatically equate to shagging him. Why do you have to see everything in terms of sex? I just don't want to leave doors closed. *You* like looking at what's behind doors. It's what you do for a living. You get in your Ford Ka and go tootling about all over the place all day long, exploring, checking everything out. I've been stuck in an office, chained to a desk, invisible for 15 years!"

"One day on set… great, yes. Do some networking; see where it leads. Just don't get carried away!"

"Who are you? My mother? I'd just quite like to

live before I get to 40! And you're the one who told me I should do a film course!"

"Okay. Point taken, Beanie. You're right. It could be useful. It's just there's something about Ossian Brohmer that I'm not too keen on... but, yeah, I guess it is an opportunity."

"*Exactly!*"

Louis opens the door.

"By the way, have you done something different to your hair?"

"Different?" says Louis, ruffling his hair, suddenly looking self-conscious. "I just didn't put any product in it, that's all. This is just the natural me."

"It's kind of like a trendy quiff. It looks better, less greasy!"

"Well, thanks for the backhanded compliment."

I take the steps down to the lobby two at a time, giggling all the way.

I enter the lobby of 2, The Promenade, with a sinking feeling. It feels shrouded in a gloomy atmosphere, a ghostly energy – that strange feeling I get, once again, from seeing the dismal trappings of a 1970s conversion superimposed on the grandeur of a past era. Somehow it feels stuck, not in the past exactly, but in a no man's land, caught between two worlds, neither of which feels in the present.

I feel an angst, deep in the pit of my stomach, to

see that I've missed three calls from Simon. No texts. I check my laptop. No emails. I immediately try ringing him, using my landline. There's no reply. It should be about midday in Cape Cod. I gaze out to sea, to the skyline where the grey tanker is still in view, as small as a plastic military miniature. If *Waking the Dead* hadn't been happening, everything would have been simple. I would have been here, waiting for the call. Or I could have gone to *Waking the Dead* still, and everything would have been fine if Ossian hadn't been there. Is there anyone else on the planet who could have distracted me from being back here, at least by morning? Maybe the answer is practical, not philosophical. It's not necessarily an existential test. I could have just taken my mobile phone with me, after all.

I text: *Dear Simon, so sorry to have missed your calls. I ended up going to this thing called Chambre Magique all night and falling asleep this morning! I hope you had a gr8 journey + am really looking fwd to catching up with you. Xx*

Then I email Belinda Dixey:
To: belinda.dixey@officesprites.com

Dear Belinda

I'm so sorry I won't be available until Tuesday. I'm so sorry about this but the opportunity of a lifetime has just arisen – work experience on the set of Ossian Brohmer's latest film. As this is something I hope to do in the future, I hope you understand. My sincere apologies. Perhaps I can do some overtime Tuesday-Friday to make up the lost time?

Sabina Upsell

I press 'send' and my laptop makes a whooshing sound as my message is dispatched to Office Sprites.

Now I've absolved myself, I shower off the salt water from my swim. I put on pyjamas and set the alarm for 5am. I sit up in bed with my laptop on my knees and type, "Ossian – latest film" into Google. Numerous articles and websites appear in the search list.

I click on *Contribute and participate in Ossian Brohmer's latest film noir, 'The Warehouse'*, and a 'Go Fund Me' page opens, which showcases Ossian in a black and white photo. The image must be from a while ago as his face is younger, smoother, and his hair still blonde. He's wearing a black leather jacket, and has a pair of dark glasses hooked in the 'V' of his T-shirt. Facing the camera, he makes a frame with his hands, as though putting the viewer in shot. The image is slightly distorted by the flash of white from an adjustable, tripod lamp, which is also facing the viewer, adding to the sense that you're dazzled, star-struck.

Greetings from Ossian Brohmer!

Nordic noir infiltrates the shores of Britain!

An opportunity to collaborate with an internationally-renowned, award-winning filmmaker on his Gothic thriller 'The Warehouse' – a tale of displacement and psychological fears, set in the City of London and the dark, flat wilderness of the Kent marshes and Dungeness.

For £50, you will be rewarded with a VIP pass to the premiere and a special mention on Ossian's Twitter page.

£100 buys you an invite to the premiere, after-party and signed photos from the cast.

Be a movie star! For just £200 you get the opportunity to be an extra with a speaking part.

For £500, spend a day on set, shadowing the award-winning Director, as well as receiving all the luscious lovely benefits mentioned above.

I scroll down to 'Comments':

"For £500, you get to kiss Ossian Brohmer's arse! ☺"

"But what's it about? Has he actually got a screenplay yet?"

"I don't understand why u're giving this talented film-maker such a hard time. Personally, I'm in! I'm actually going to be in a movie! It's something to show the grand-kids when u're like 80 years old!"

"I agree. It makes a unique birthday or Christmas present for someone who's really into film."

"Sounds like shit."

"Fuck u."

"Ossian Brohmer is a douchebag."

"Go fund Ossian Brohmer's drug habit. ☜"

My eyes widen as I go down the list. I click my laptop shut, feeling too tired to read the full snake of verbiage. I lie in the dark, stabbed with disappointment to see Ossian treated with such irreverence. It's just the jealousy of people with non-lives, people who don't know how to be creative themselves. Online trolls. Hiding behind the Internet from the comfort of their own homes. Fine, if you want to create a well-structured article and put it in a newspaper. But this is the problem with the Internet. All you need to do is tap out the letters "F-u-c-k u" with two fingers and it's on the World Wide Web for all to read. Okay, he takes the odd drug, drinks, whatever. That's what artistic types do. I check back in my mind, the image of Ossian on the beach, swimming in the sea, healthy – good-looking, even. Hardly a druggie. I re-conjure the image of the ship's medicine cabinet. Not entirely conventional, admittedly. But, like Lola said, *controlled*. At the end of the day, Ossian is *controlled*.

And the screenplay. *Has* he written the screenplay? I'd always fancied having a go at writing a movie. Maybe not by myself. Not the blank page. But a collaboration. Yes, I'd still like to go up to The Pineapple and give it a good clean. I like cleaning, actually. But now, for some reason, I'm seeing myself at an awards ceremony. Okay, not necessarily the Oscars, but a film awards ceremony. Walking down the red carpet with Ossian. And then we're seated around one of those round tables – me dressed in an off-the-shoulder designer gown, Ossian in a tuxedo – with glasses of champagne, when it's announced: "Best Screenplay – Ossian Brohmer and Beanie Upsell for *The Warehouse!*"

2 2

On Location, Darling

"Where the hell is Faye Morrison?" demands Ossian.

Faye Morrison is playing the role of Julia. Ossian is a bit stressed as we're already running late. The Morris Minor broke down on the way to London. As well as Pixie, Lola and I in the car, there was also Roo, a photographer, who's just moved to Quinton-on-Sea and who Ossian had recruited to take some arty location shots. Anyway, we had to wait at the roadside for the AA to come and fix something under the bonnet. Spark plugs or something. The AA guy checked the oil and water and told Ossian off as they needed filling up and then added that vintage cars were okay as a local run-around but he'd be better off getting a more modern car for longer journeys.

"Christ!" said Ossian, as we finally pulled away. "His job is to fix the car, not give me a bloody lecture! And, no, I don't want to drive around in some bloody modern bland-mobile! If I want to drive a bloody computer I can go into the amusement arcade on Quinton seafront and play Storm Raider or whatever it's called."

"Storm *Rider*."

"You know it? Don't tell me you've been going in there playing bloody Storm Raider, Lola!"

"Hey, Ossian! Chill!"

"Stop being a back-seat driver!"

"I'm not being a back-seat driver! I'm just saying 'Chill!'"

Lola leant forward and started massaging Ossian's shoulders and I noticed that he broke out into a smile. Annoyingly, I felt a speck of… not jealousy, exactly. It's just that I felt a bit repressed compared to Lola's carefree confidence. I also told myself be prepared for the fact that Ossian's London girlfriend might show up on set. It's not that I want to be Ossian's girlfriend (at least, I don't think so), but I was aware of the fact that I'd feel less special once a confident, model-type was around.

"I know fuck all about engines, but I do like to be able to see what's what when I open the bonnet. Physical things. Fan belts and what not. I could be really British, put on a boiler suit, join a Morris Minor owners' club and learn how to fix the thing myself!"

Pixie laughed "No you couldn't!" Then Pixie and Lola both burst into laughter – literally collapsed into one another in cascades of giggles. I wondered if they were showing off in front of Roo because he's so stylish and good-looking.

"Morris Minor owners' club!"

Then Roo joined in, "And where's your tartan blanket? You're supposed to have a tartan blanket on the back seat!"

"Ha, ha, ha! Very funny!" complained Ossian.

So, we're doing screen tests of a scene that takes place in the headquarters of an international bank near Liverpool Street. It feels strange to be back in this familiar city setting on a busy Monday, and yet to be free, not chained to a desk. From the high-rise building we're in (on the third floor) I can see directly into the windows of other offices, where workers sit in cubicles. They have cause to get up from time to time, but mostly they're in their cubicles – of which I can practically see the minutiae, from where I stand, metres away: the updated staff lists, with their speed dial numbers; the client contact lists. I can see piles of buff-coloured foolscap files stacked to one side, which is a dead give-away that it's a law firm. One man stands at the glass wall looking out holding a Dictaphone, into which he speaks rapidly. I'm standing here in my jeans and T-shirt, with this feeling that I've skipped school.

I'm not sure what my role is here. I just observe the technological paraphernalia, and the crew setting it up, with a sense of awe: the sound boom, the cameras on tripods, the lights.

"We literally just had a call," says Lola. "Faye was stuck on an underground train in Balham for half an hour. She's at Embankment right now. She'll be another 40 minutes?"

"Let's get moving," says Ossian. He claps his hands.

"Beanie, would you read the part of Julia to fill in for the moment?"

This is ridiculous. How can I have gone from sitting

in an office cubicle for 15 years, to being on location with the director of *The Index of Dreams*, to now being asked to read the female lead? Even though it's only a rehearsal, the cameras will be rolling. Despite being in the age of ubiquitous cameras, I've lived under a rock. The only footage of me is a few seconds in a DVD of my sister's wedding. Once more, I'm riding the crest of the wave, I'm watching the flower petals unfurl. I'm stepping onto the stage. My years of hiding have made me hungry for the chance, even though I'm just a stand-in for a few minutes.

"I've never acted," I say.

"No worries. Just read from the script."

"Okay."

"Great. So, Beanie, you're here."

Ossian guides me over to the reception desk where the character Julia is supposed to sit. The character is an office worker. It's not like I'm being asked to play a gang leader with an East End accent. Lola steps in and hands me the appropriate pages. She's already highlighted the relevant dialogue in fluorescent green.

"So basically, Julia – that's you – is a receptionist during the graveyard shift at some international bank. This is not by any means the highpoint of her life. She's just come back from abroad, broken hearted, after missing an opportunity to be with someone who was her soulmate. She's just about had enough. Of the office. Of London. Of life. She's having a crap time at work, she lives in a shitty basement flat in some God-forsaken part of London, she's in debt, she's got no friends and it's dawning on her that her life is absolutely pointless. Totally meaningless. She's met a guy recently and he feels the same way. They've had enough of life… that's their shared ground. Okay?"

I nod. "I can understand Julia feeling that way," I say. "I've been there myself."

Ossian looks at me. His eyes feel as if they penetrate my soul. "Mmm, I had a feeling you might have done." He carries on staring at me for a few more moments and then, waving the script pages, continues on with his directions.

"So, in this scene, Martin, played by Dean, that guy over there with the goatee, is her boss, a real bastard, and he's been out drinking with his secretary, Sasha, who's played by Pixie. Basically, they come back to the office, completely out of their heads. The lift doors are going to ping open and out come Dean and Pixie, pissed, and start giving you a hard time. That's it, basically! Okay? Relax! It's only a rehearsal! It's only a test-run! Okay? Okay! Quiet on set!"

There's a camera focussed on me. *Me.* The sound boom, the fluffy thing on a pole that I've sometimes seen when walking past film-sets, is held towards me. Lola and another girl are in the background, holding clipboards. Ossian takes a look through the camera lens, adjusts something and murmurs a few final words of instruction to the cameraman.

A mobile phone starts ringing – with the ring-tone of *Bedshaped*.

"Hey, basics!" says Ossian. "Mobile phones off! Whose phone is that?"

"Sorry!" I say. "Just one sec."

I run over to my bag. Two missed calls it says on the screen. Right now, I don't want to think about who they might be from. I switch it off and run back to the reception desk.

"Okay!" says Ossian again. "Quiet on set!"

All I know is I'm going to say the words. That, and the fact that I want to do it. I'm stepping out off the edge of a cliff. But I want to do it.

"Speed!" says the sound engineer.

"Rolling!" says the cameraman.

"Action!" says Ossian.

INT. RECEPTION. NIGHT

The lift doors open and MARTIN and SASHA walk in. MARTIN is unsteady on his feet. SASHA comes up to reception. MARTIN heads into the Gents.

SASHA
(slurring)
Martin wants to talk to you. Now.

JULIA
Now?

SASHA
Now this minute. He's very upset with you. Your time is up.

MARTIN comes out of the Gents, walks past reception, making no eye contact.

MARTIN
(slurring)
My office. Now.

JULIA
Whatever you've got to say, just say it here.

MARTIN ignores her and disappears into his office. JULIA leaves the reception desk and follows him.

Ossian says, "Cut! Good! Let's go straight into the next scene. So Dean, you walk into your office and stand by the door. Beanie, you walk through the door. Dean, you slam the door shut. We'll just keep the cameras rolling. It's supposed to be night. Just pretend it's night. It's only a rehearsal. Okay! Action!"

I ready myself to step off the cliff once more. I'm ready to step into thin air again.

INTERIOR. MARTIN'S OFFICE. NIGHT

MARTIN slams the door shut. JULIA walks to the desk and sits in the spare chair. The office is dark, save for the light coming from a small desk lamp.

MARTIN walks across to the desk and, holding the back of Julia's chair, leans down and talks into her ear.

MARTIN
(*slurring*)
I am very disappointed in you. Very. Disappointed. I rang the office on business just now. You put the phone down on me.

JULIA
You rang from a bar. Drunk. Abusive.

MARTIN stands up and walks round to his seat, slumps into it and leans heavily forward on the desk.

MARTIN
I'm informing you that I'll be discussing the termination of your employment at EC Banking with HR in the morning. If you want to keep your employment with us, which I'm sure is very much the case…

JULIA
(*Laughing, wryly.*)
Even if you were talking sense, do you really think I'd give a toss about this job? It's you I feel sorry for. This is it. You've never experienced anything else. Just this.
(*gesturing to his office and the city beyond the window*)

This is all you know.

MARTIN

I am warning you to watch what you say. If you
imagine you can…

JULIA
(Interrupting)

You think you're so important. Martin Hullington. Ex-
ecutive. A real smart arse who thinks he knows exactly
where he's going. That the real meaning of life is to
become a top trader at EC Banking by age 35, have 2.4
kids and put photos of them all around his office…

MARTIN

Given the choice between that and being a
buttoned-up, spinster receptionist…

JULIA turns back to look out of the window, across
the lit-up city.

JULIA

All of this means nothing to me. You don't have a clue
about me. You don't know what the natural world is.

MARTIN
(Angry)

What the hell are you doing here, that's what I want to
know? Why don't you bugger off back to your natural
world if it's so great there? You're wasting my ti…

JULIA
(Interrupts)
You think I'd be here if I had the choice?
(Looking into the distance)
Sometimes you just take the wrong fork in the road…

MARTIN
Well, you bloody well don't belong here.

JULIA
(Standing up)
I'm GLAD I don't belong here!

JULIA looks at MARTIN, shakes her head and laughs. Then she turns and walks out of his office.

Ossian waves an arm in the air. "Cut! Great!"

Ossian says we're going to film the same scene from my point of view and then from Martin's point of view, and then we film it again, doing close-ups. So I get to be Julia, I get to have the camera on me, all over again x 3. Again, amidst the pleasure is a pinprick of pain – for the glimpse of what life can be, of the kind of life that some people live all the time. The pinprick of pain for the fact I'm back at a desk tomorrow; that I'll be typing in the police station – if they haven't withdrawn the contract due to my absence today, that is.

The festive feeling, the feeling that life is fun, continues into the lunch-hour, when the crew head en masse to an Italian restaurant that Ossian knows just around the corner, "that does a fabulous two-course meal for £10."

I worked in this area for years, but I never knew about the fabulous Italian restaurant 'just around the corner'. I walk along the pavement, in the sunshine, feeling almost guilty that I'm not snatching a sandwich and a packet of crisps from Pret A Manger and then rushing back to my desk.

At the restaurant we sit down altogether around a large table. Ossian is keen to sit next to me and reseats Pixie, because he wants to do a 'recce' on the morning's events.

"You're a very good actress. Hasn't anyone ever told you before?"

"I told you! I haven't acted before. Though, yes, someone did once tell me I was a very good actress." I lower my voice. "I was in a hospital when I was sixteen. I'd taken some paracetamols. Well, quite a lot, actually."

"You tried to kill yourself?"

"Yes. And so this psychiatrist says to me, 'You're a very good actress.' Because I was acting matter-of-fact about it. When I had to talk about it, she said I could have been talking about anything – a trip to the cinema, a walk by a river; I talked about it cheerfully. But I was just being myself. I wasn't acting."

"You're a tough cookie."

Under the table, he touches my hand – perhaps as a sign of empathy, sympathy or whatever because of my teenage incident. At least he doesn't say anything really annoying, like, "Do you ever feel like that now?" or, even more annoying, "You need help."

I look across the table to where Roo, Lola and Pixie are sitting. I can't help notice how they have a more composed look on their face when they're addressing Roo – compared to when they're talking to Ossian. Basically, I can tell they take Roo more seriously than Ossian, which seems strange to me, because Ossian is *Ossian* and although Roo is stylishly cool with his hint of a trendy quiff, he's just a photographer. But it's fair enough, really. They see Roo as a *prospect*, whereas maybe they regard Ossian as outside of their age category.

Then Roo's addressing me. "Didn't I see you at The Candy Box the other night?"

"I *was* there the other night. Friday night."

"You were with… weren't you with this guy who was wearing a cool flowery tie?"

"That's right!"

"*With* a guy?" asks Ossian. "Are you harbouring a secret boyfriend, Beanie?"

"Not exactly *a boyfriend*. But I had a date!"

"And this date… this seed, if you like," presses Ossian, "…is it sprouting? Flourishing?"

"I'm not quite sure! He just had to go away for two weeks!"

I go outside and check who was ringing earlier. Simon. He must have been ringing at what was the middle of the night for him. There's a text from Belinda Dixey, assuring me that the HR department were 'very understanding' about my sudden absence and that they are expecting me at 9am tomorrow.

⁂

I spend the afternoon watching Faye Morrison play the role of Julia in the rehearsals. Of course, I end up wondering if she's better than me. Ossian gives me a role as continuity supervisor, which means that if, say, a glass of water is full at the beginning of a scene, but half drunk by the end of the scene, then when they re-do the scene, say, from another angle, you have to make sure the glass is full again at the beginning. I find it hard to keep track, and another crew member keeps stepping in and saying things like, "Hang on a minute, I just need to put the jacket back on the chair," etcetera. By 5pm I'm flagging and when Roo announces to Ossian that he's hopping on a train back to Quinton as he's got a dinner party to go to later, there's a part of me that wants to call it quits as well.

I feel my old insecurities creeping in. Am I tired? Is it the contrast to my earlier role? Have the last vestiges of Saturday night's E worn off? I'm glad when it's 7pm and Ossian calls it "a wrap".

We're on the way home, in his racing green Morris Minor (Ossian and I in the front and Pixie and Lola in the back), with The Clash blaring from the tape deck. I wind down the window and enjoy the balmy breeze of summer's end and the way the speed of the car makes the wind rush through my hair, blowing it across my face – making me feel, almost, like the model in the photo in Ossian's kitchen, standing with him by the private jet, their hair tossed in the air.

Ossian is saying something, bringing me back to the present moment. I strain to hear his words above the horn section of *Rudie Can't Fail*. He says something like: "You know what you said earlier... about... I was wondering, do you still have those feelings?"

In the midst of my pleasant reverie, I'm not quite sure what he means. All I know is I feel great – whether earlier or now, despite my exhaustion, I still feel great. I turn to Ossian with a little smile – a smile of gratitude for everything. He seems serious, the look on his face expectant, like he's really listening out for my answer.

"Sure," I say, and turn back to the window, where the wind and the sun catch my face and make me feel wild, alive.

I have to admit, my feelings about the day have changed *slightly* by the time we enter the driveway of The Pineapple at around midnight. We were somewhere along the A2 when Ossian announced, "How about a bite to eat?" as he pulled over into a modern, red-brick roadside inn. A large sign in the car-park advertised some of the fare on offer: chips, cola in disposable cups, and deep-fried items that screamed out with radioactive brightness in the dusk.

"What? In here?" asked Lola.

"Sure, why not?"

"Why *not*?!" exclaimed Pixie. "To be brutally honest, Ozz, I don't think you'll like it in there."

"All I'm saying is let's unwind for half an hour!"

"Okay, Ozz, you're the boss!"

Dutifully, we followed Ossian through the glass swing doors and traipsed along a sticky, zany carpet with a geometric design, the kind that is favoured in cinemas and casinos. A surround-sound system belted out classic love anthems on a loop. Songs like *Everything I do* by Bryan Adams and *Rule The World* by Take That.

Once we'd got our gin and tonics from the bar, we headed to the dining area. The blue fabric chairs were slightly stained, but I guess the management didn't need to worry about that as the restaurant was fairly busy with families and couples taking advantage of the two-for-one deals.

Ossian opened the large, laminated menu. "When in Rome... I think I'll have chicken nuggets and chips."

"Chicken nuggets? You know why the chicken's so cheap?" remonstrated Pixie. "I keep getting these video clips because I 'liked' PETA on Facebook. Next thing I know, I'm checking my newsfeed late at night when I can't sleep, you know, for a bit of late-night comfort, and *suddenly* this PETA video comes up... all these chickens piled like rubbish, hobbling..."

"Stop! I don't want to know the details! I don't *need* to know the details. I don't eat chicken!" Lola cut in.

Ossian raised his hands in surrender, "Okay! Fine! I *won't* have the chicken nuggets!"

"You can still do the 'when in Rome' thing... there's plenty to choose from. Onion rings, French fries, garlic mushrooms..."

"Okay! That's fine! I'll have the onion rings and what-ever… and let's get some more G&Ts in."

I was quite drunk after two gin and tonics. Everybody became very relaxed about the 'theme park' experi-ence of the 'motel' and Ossian said it wasn't wasted; it was all research that could be used in a film. He was really relaxed. Zonked, actually, by about the fourth gin and tonic and that's when he suggested we check into the hotel.

"It's all research for my next film!"

Ossian went ahead and booked two twin rooms. Or tried to. He couldn't remember his PIN, so I stepped in and paid with my own card. It was worth it, I reasoned to myself. Cheap at the price. A day on set with Ossian Brohmer. £160. Cheap at the price, really. I had to mention to Ossian that I'd kind of been planning an early start in Quinton the next day. I didn't want to reveal I was working at the police station, so it was tricky to explain my exact circumstances. But he seemed keen to defer to me, especially now that I'd paid for the rooms.

"Oh don't worry about that. They serve breakfast from 5am. We'll be out of here by 6!"

Ossian took the keys from the receptionist and said he'd rejoin us in the restaurant in a minute.

Ossian took it for granted that we'd be sharing a room, which was fine – no big deal. After all, we'd even shared a bed before. At 10.30pm, feeling exhausted, I went to crash out before the others. Ossian gave me the key with its large orange plastic tab that had the room number on it.

So, there I was in this functional room, without a toothbrush or any spare clothes. I guess it didn't matter. As long as we did actually leave by 6am – or even 7 – everything would be fine. I went through to the en suite bathroom, stared at myself in the mirror and asked myself whether I really wanted to be here. What were we doing in this motel just off the A2? I was just putting a tampon wrapper in the bathroom bin when I noticed something in the bottom of the bin's plastic bag. It was a tall, thin bin, designed so that any detritus deposited within it would end up out of view. But I was surprised that it hadn't been emptied. And that's when I noticed. It was a used needle. Perhaps a diabetic's used needle. Who was to say?

When I casually mentioned the needle to Ossian when he staggered up to the room later on, he insisted on taking issue with the management. Caused a row. Said it was unacceptable and that we wanted a refund for the whole evening and that we were leaving. The receptionist insisted that the rooms were checked over routinely every morning. "I can assure you, sir, that we have very high standards."

"I don't care!" remonstrated Ossian, "We're off!"

Then the receptionist asked, "Are you yourself the driver, sir? Are you safe to drive, sir?" and this caused even more of a rumpus.

Normally, I wouldn't have offered – to drive, that is. I mean, I hadn't driven in about 17 years. But there was something about being in front of the camera that morning that had put me on a high, given me a rush of adrenaline, a feeling that anything was possible.

"I've got a driving licence," I proffered. "If you've got fully comprehensive insurance, I can drive your car. At least, I think so… And I haven't driven for ages, but…"

"Comprehensive? Yes, sure," said Ossian. "Let's just go."

After calling the manager to the front desk, the receptionist was authorised to give a refund straight back onto my debit card and then we left.

Suddenly, I was the grown-up, in the driving seat. My brother had once given me a few driving lessons in my granny's old Mini before I passed my test (on the sixth go) in a more modern car. I fiddled with the switches to reacquaint myself with the lights, indicators and so forth. Then I went through the drill "neutral – engine – clutch – into first – gas – check mirror, release handbrake." Then miraculously, we were off.

We were tootling along the A2 without incident when a police car passed by.

"Shit!" I exclaimed.

"Why? You're doing great!" said Pixie. "You might get stopped for going too slowly… they might think something's wrong, that you need help! But apart from that, you're doing great!"

I dropped Pixie and Lola off at the flat they share in the old town and then, by the time we rolled through the gates of The Pineapple, it was around midnight. Ossian was so tired he almost seemed drugged, so I accompanied him into the cottage to ensure that he was able to stagger safely upstairs to bed.

Then I walked home, taking the main road rather than going via the beach. I wound my way down the hill with this niggling feeling. I mean, I still wanted to be on set with him and things like that, but perhaps I didn't *need* Ossian in quite the way I had once imagined. In a strange way, it felt like a loss.

23

The Police Station

After the rollercoaster of the last few days, there's something almost reassuring about just being able to touch base for a while. Sitting typing at the police station gives me a chance to catch my breath, and get paid at the same time. I'm typing up PACE (Police and Criminal Evidence) witness statements and interviews, with a sense that it's good to ground myself. My anxiety about Office Sprites is resolved with each tap on the keyboard. I'm here now, doing what I said I would do. I don't want to go sailing off into the sunset of glamorous possibilities until I've completed the task, absolved myself. After all, sailing off towards excitement could be an illusion, a balloon that's popped overnight. I do want to sail off and explore, I just need to keep one foot on the ground. After all, I'm not a giddy teenager. Somehow, I manage to think all these thoughts while I tap away at the keyboard, underneath the de rigueur fluorescent office lighting.

It's slightly annoying that they've put the heating on.

I want to open the window, but one of the secretaries says she's cold and I'm quickly reminded, all over again, why I can never envisage my future in a place like this. I'm reminded that the secretarial species seem keen on cooking themselves in high temperatures, even when it's sunny outside. There's a radio on in the room belting out the kind of pop-tastic music favoured by DJ Topsie Smith, except that the radio DJ's chatter is just totally inane, talking about the fact that it's so-and-so's birthday or wedding anniversary, followed by jingles and an advert for a local cement company or a local storage company or whatever. I find it strange they've got a radio on as, even when you've got the headphones on to transcribe, you can still vaguely hear its tinny, relentless whine in the background.

I haven't typed for a long time. It's almost like my fingers need the exercise. I gallop through pages of photocopied, handwritten statements, pausing only to decipher strange spellings and cramped, illegible letters. I transcribe the words of taped interviews, voices of strangers that grip me in the midst of their fear, defiance or keenness to co-operate. It's interesting when someone mentions a street I've heard of. A particular street is mentioned several times, and I make a mental note to be wary of ever living there. Surfaces are peeled away and I enter a twilight world that involves petty theft, rewiring electricity circuits away from meters, assault and a gruesome case of grievous bodily harm. As I finish each job I return to the main list and click on the next one to be typed, processed and computerised. In turn, I tick each one as finished on the computerised list, with a sense of efficiency – the efficiency of being a cog in the crime-processing conveyor-belt.

It's true that the work isn't boring, at least. And there's a kettle on a tray, with boxes of tea bags and a jar of instant coffee where we can help ourselves to a drink. I make myself a mint tea, wincing slightly at the trace of sour-milk smell in the mug. There are four of us at the work-stations, tap-tap-tapping away, and an older lady with a swirl of dyed mahogany-coloured hair swept up into a bun on the top of her head, who sits in an annexe, just to one side. Next to her is the basket with the photo-copied statements for copy typing, and the tapes, with instruction sheets attached, for transcribing.

On the stroke of 12.30pm, the official start of lunchtime, my trigger-impatient fingers tap onto the Internet to check my email. With a jolt, I see the name 's.beresford' in my inbox with the subject heading 'Finally Connected'; involuntarily, a burst of energy implodes through my circulatory system – involuntarily, because, with Ossian Brohmer making dreams come true, how can anything else stand a chance?

Dearest Sabina

I'm here on a pocket of Nantucket Island with the worst Internet connection ever. I kept trying to send emails from my iPhone without any luck. So, finally, have found an Internet café with a connection.

To be honest, although it's beautiful here, I keep thinking how much more I'd enjoy it with your company. I miss your smiling cat face. I looked up the name 'Sabina' and see that it has a connection to the Egyptian word for 'cat'.

I hope you're having a wonderful time in Quinton-on-Sea. Thanks for your news re. Chambre Magique. Perhaps you could introduce me to Chambre Magique, it sounds fascinating.

I'll come back to the café to send another message very soon.

Thinking about you – quite a lot!

Simon x

I look out the window at the dark grey rain clouds and the rather uninspiring view of the unmarked, dark blue police vehicles at the back of the building, with the feeling that it doesn't matter at all that I'm not sitting in a beautiful place. There is that sense of a sudden wave lifting me off my feet, the high tide, the pebbles beneath you shelving away, so that you're no longer on solid ground, but floating. On the warm surface, the light sparkles. Below is the unknown, the letting go, the being lifted by a force that is larger. I'll reply later, when I have time to think, time to find the perfect words, and sleep with drops of cedarwood oil on my pillow.

When my reverie finally comes to an end, I notice that, strangely, in my inbox there's another new email.

To: S Upsell
From: Ossian Brohmer
Subject: Photos!

Dear Beanie

Hey! Well done for getting everything sorted yesterday ☺
Look! Great photos! I hope you don't mind, I'm going to post
some of these on Facebook and on my website!

Ossian

I click the attachment open: a series of photos taken on
set yesterday. It's me, but I look different. I'm caught up
in the moment, unaware of the camera. There's one where
everyone, the whole crew, is posing in an end-of-the-
day, wrap shot. I'm next to Ossian, tucked into his arm,
amongst the crowd. The amazing thing is, there isn't a
single bad, self-conscious photo. I even think about reac-
tivating my Facebook account so I can post them online
and give the appearance that my life has become really
exciting. Well, it has been really exciting, in reality, for
at least the last few days. And somehow the photos make
the experience official, substantial; even if it's just in my
eyes, they make me seem a different person. As though,
almost, I'm an actress now. Or, I've 'got acting experience'. Just think, if someone Googled me, and this was
all they saw, they'd get completely the wrong impression.
Invisible life is invisible, so the 15 years trapped in an
office is undetectable. And then, just the three hours of

me as Julia, on set with Ossian Brohmer, is what people would see.

One of the secretaries, Penny, passes behind my desk. "Sorry to be nosy. Is that you? Are you an actress?"

"Not exactly," I say.

"Are you just doing this as a filler-in?"

"Kind of."

"Is that the film director who lives up on the cliffs?"

"Yes. It's Ossian Brohmer."

"Really? I saw him once. I walked into The White Hart and he was sitting there with some friends. He's drop-dead gorgeous. Don't you think?"

"It's true; he is."

The older lady with the swirl of mahogany hair – whose name, I can now see on her security pass, is Maureen – raises her eyebrows and smiles with surprise. "Ah! You know him?" she says, "He once made a really interesting film, didn't he?"

I'm feeling very hungry and, apart from an apple in my bag, I haven't brought any food and have to rely on a sandwich from the vending machine in the corridor. I stand there for about five minutes, wondering whether I can stomach the white-sliced bread with grated cheese and mayonnaise or the dry-looking dyed-brown bread with slices of hard-boiled egg and irradiated tomato. In the end, I break my no-tuna rule and opt for the tuna mayonnaise and cucumber baguette. I sit on a banquette in a corner of the large 'club room' with the other secretaries. A television flickers with the lunchtime news. There's a bar to one side and a large pool table. I wonder what would happen if you were a police officer and you wanted to go to something like Chambre Magique.

Would you turn a blind eye if you're standing outside and someone offers you a toke on a joint or a pill? What if you find yourself standing next to someone you interviewed last week? Maybe that's why they have to have 'the club room'. Maybe they have parties here, away from awkward possibilities.

One of the secretaries giggles and mentions she's "been out clubbing, non-stop." Since Chambre Magique, I'm sure that 'clubbing' is shorthand for taking E and dancing. I'm bursting with excitement to mention my experience at the weekend and to ask her if she takes E, but manage to reign myself in. Instead, I bask in their questions about Ossian Brohmer.

"Have you actually been to his house?"

"Are you actually going to be in one of his films?"

"Does he have a girlfriend?"

It's almost too much reflected glory to take in. Perhaps it's a little too magnified, a little too dangerous, that two-and-a-half days of my life can start mushrooming out of control and obliterate everything else.

Luckily, I'm heading to the loo when he rings – luckily, because I'm falsely elevated enough already in the eyes of the secretaries – elevated as someone with a glamorous life. It's pleasant, but for it to increase any further, by actually taking a call from Ossian in front of them, would be just taking it too far, like I was his girlfriend or something.

I'm standing by the hand-dryer and the bin of used paper-towels in the loos, in the belly of Quinton police station, when I take the call.

"Hello?" I use an interrogative lilt, even though it's perfectly clear from my mobile screen that it's Ossian calling.

"Beanie! It's me, it's Ossian!"

"Oh, hi! Thank you for the photos."

"Terrific photos. Oh, and by the way, well done for being the chauffeur last night! You're a right little Herbie!"

"Herbie?"

"*Herbie Rides Again? Herbie Goes to Monte Carlo*?... Anyway, I was thinking, why don't you come round to mine for afternoon coffee?"

"I'm at work."

"Work? You didn't tell me you worked!"

"Most people do. What did you think I did with my time?" I say with a laugh that sounds slightly forced.

"I don't know… something vaguely arty as an excuse for a job, like every other person in this town."

"I'm just temping in an office." I make a quick calculation whether to tell Ossian I'm working at the police station – or pig station, as Ossian would probably call it. I recall something in the tone of his voice that night – "The pigs are here! I think we need to make a move…" – that tells me not to tell him. I'm only here for a few days, after all. He doesn't actually need to ever know.

"Where?"

"At a solicitors, just doing legal secretarial work."

"But where? I could come and pick you up when you finish."

I'm like one of the suspects, caught out by police questioning. I can't not know where I'm working. One of the duty solicitors in one of the interviews said he was from a firm called something like... Baxters?

"Oh, please don't worry. I need to touch base…"

"It's pissing down with rain. I could give you a lift. Where are you?"

"Baxters? But I definitely need to head home…"

"It's just there's something I'd like to ask you. Something that would involve a short, but exciting trip." For some reason, he sounds nervous, as though short of breath. I relegate the thought to the back of my mind, because he's Ossian Brohmer and I'm Beanie Upsell. *He's* the one on the pedestal.

"Wow… okay."

"It would be great to touch base about it as I'm back on location tomorrow till Friday."

"Wow… okay."

"What time do you finish?"

"Um, 5?"

"I'll pick you up at 5pm. Where exactly is Baxters?"

"Don't worry about finding it. I'll wait for you, say, outside The Marina."

"Don't wait outside in the rain! I'll see you at 5pm. Where is Baxters?"

"It's in… I've forgotten the name of the street… I'll just go and ask one of the secretaries, hang on…"

"Don't worry, I'll Google it."

And then he rings off.

I spend the rest of the afternoon transcribing more interviews that remind me over and over why a lie is never a simple thing. It's an isolated piece of information, without context, without a network of connections. Like a suspect caught in the light, I'm wondering how I can back-track, how I can quickly try and fill in the gaps around the lie, the words that stand in isolation, this rocky outcrop from which it's easy to fall. I Google

Baxters too. It's up near the business park, about quarter of a mile away. This is like a blot on my new, starry world. Damage limitation is needed.

As I type away, I make my plan. It's quite simple, really. It's not as complicated as a James Bond film, exactly. I'm going to order a taxi at 4.45pm to take me up to the business park and I'm going to stand outside Baxters. If it's still pouring with rain, I'll go into the reception and ask them about their conveyancing fees, etcetera, and linger over the inevitable leaflets in reception about why you should make a Will etcetera. And when I see Ossian's Morris Minor outside, then I'll step out. It will be quite simple, really.

Of course, I'll need to also explain why I'm leaving work early. I'll think of something nearer the time. Perhaps, as the secretaries and Maureen, the supervisor with the mahogany-swirl hair, are so nice, I could even tell them the truth: that I wasn't sure of protocol with new acquaintances – about whether you tell them you're at The Police Station – and now I'm in a pickle. That I wasn't quite sure just how far The Official Secrets Act extended into your actual life.

The easiest thing would be to clear up this mess with Ossian, too. Just tell him, for goodness sake, as soon as I get in the car: actually I was working at the police station, but I just had the impression you didn't like the police, so I lied. I got myself in a tangle and now I need to untangle it.

24

One Size Fits All

I stand outside Baxters, sheltering in the large entranceway, at 4.50pm. We finished work at 4.30pm anyway, so I've walked up here, after all. Walked in the pouring rain, which continues to shower me as it drives at an angle. By 5.05pm I wonder whether Ossian's car wouldn't start or something, so I look at my mobile but there's only one bar showing on the signal. Maybe he couldn't get through and he's had to ring Baxters to ask them to tell me he's going to be late.

From where I'm standing, I can see the receptionist at her desk on the other side of the large, plate-glass doors. I feel panicky as I imagine her saying, "Who?" Then she'll buzz through to Human Resources and they'll confirm there is no temp working for them called Sabina Upsell. Then, when she confirms to Ossian I'm definitely unknown to them, Ossian will think I'm one of those strange people who pretend they've got a job when they haven't, like that French guy who pretended he was a doctor for 18 years and 'set off for work every day', but spent his time sitting in his car or in libraries, reading medical journals. I work myself into such a panic that I glance through the window again to the receptionist to see if she seems perturbed in any way, like she's received any kind of bizarre phone call, but she looks perfectly calm, sees me looking in and even gives me a polite smile.

This is so ridiculous that I think I'm going to confess my lie to Ossian, after all, as soon as he arrives; but then he turns up in his green Morris Minor, looking perfectly happy. I open the passenger door.

"You're soaked! Get in! Sorry I'm late, I was in the middle of a phone call. So… the multi-talented Beanie Upsell," he says, "Actress-come-legal secretary."

"That's right!" I laugh.

"I like the look," he says.

"The wet look?"

"The secretarial look. But yes, you're wet. How did you get so completely soaked?"

"Here," says Ossian, tossing some leggings, a T-shirt and a couple of jumpers out of the drawer that contains his ex's clothes. "What would you like? Valentino? Miu Miu? Izzy Lane? A pair of leggings from Comme des Garcons?" he says, looking at the labels. "Leggings are good, they're kind of one-size-fits-all. And next time they ask you to go to the post box in the pouring rain, just tell them to bugger off or to DIY. Do It Yourself. I would have thought those sorts of places had a postal van collection, anyway. And sue them if you come down with a cold."

I take the pile of clothes into the bathroom, where he's run me a bath in an old iron tub with claw feet. There's a bit of a 'high tide' mark where the hard water has stained the thin enamel coating, but it feels quite comforting, like the vestige of a time before the world went refurbishment mad. I close the bathroom door, undress and sink into the hot water, thinking it feels a bit domestic, rather cosy and familiar, pleasant, to be having a bath and changing clothes at Ossian's house. As though I'm his girlfriend or something.

Afterwards, I put on the sparkly velour leggings. They smell a little bit musty, but they're nice. I could get an appetite for designer clothes. There's a Comme des Garcons sweatshirt as well, but it has the words 'Fuckdown' on it for some reason, so I opt for the Izzy Lane ethical cashmere, red V-necked sweater instead. The clothes feel rather fine, soft, and I wonder if there's any chance I can keep them. In fact, it would be really tempting to go through the whole drawer and unburden Ossian of any unwanted items.

The feeling that I'm in a kind of lock-down of domestic arrangement continues in the kitchen where Ossian presents me with a plate of cheese soufflé and green salad, and a tall-stemmed glass of chilled white wine. It's a very pleasant lock-down, a very pleasant sensation, as far as unplanned domestic situations go. I remind myself to let go into the moment. If I'm to be an artistic person, I need to float on the wave and let go of all the conditioning about what this means or that means. That's the allure of the theatrical types – they know how to carry it off, to not take things too seriously.

25

An Invitation

Ossian paces around the kitchen, in a slightly agitated manner, then throws down a dusky pink card, onto the kitchen table:

> *Say it ain't so!*
> *Honey Gardener is gonna be the big 4-0!!*
> *Honey cordially invites Ossian Brohmer plus guest*
> *To her birthday party at Ammonite's, King's Road, SW3*
> *Friday 11th September 8pm until late*

The Ammonite? In my mind's eye I see the black and white photos of socialites, aristocrats and la crème de la crème of the rock world standing against its flock wallpaper in the sixties and seventies – and, perhaps in more recent times, on stylish sofas in the bar. The Ammonite…

usually, getting access to the famous nightclub is harder than passing through the eye of a needle – unless you're very rich and well connected, that is.

"Have you ever been to The Green Ground in Chelsea?"

I haven't even heard of The Green Ground – in Chelsea or anywhere else.

"No." I wonder if it's a tennis club, a bowling green or some kind of eco-business.

"My philosophy is, if you're going to stay somewhere, stay somewhere nice. I know people who travel to the other side of the world and they book into a hotel that's like the One Star Motel in Wolverhampton. I'd rather go for a couple of nights somewhere that's really – what do you call it – the dog's bollocks?"

"It sounds nice."

"So, anyway, that's what I wanted to ask you. Are you in on this little trip?"

"It sounds amazing. I'd be crazy to say 'no'!"

"So, what I was thinking… I pick you up on Friday. We drive up to ye olde London town and check in at The Green Ground, which is just around the corner from The Ammonite."

"Wow. It's like a dream scenario."

"That's exactly what I want it to be."

Ossian sits down on the chair next to me. "I really, really want this to be like our own *Index of Dreams*. Do you know what I mean?" His voice sounds tight, like it did on the phone earlier.

"I think so. But why me? You could invite anyone!"

Suddenly, he slumps, his head in his hands, and then looks back up.

"But that's just it, Beanie. It can't just be any one. I thought I'd met someone to have the ultimate dream with, but she went off on her own. She let me down. She went off on her own. I'm tired, Beanie, tired of everything. It just seems like the right time."

The right time… to…? To go to a party? To stay at a hotel? It does seem like a good time to go. Friday night, the end of a busy week. But he seems to be driving at something bigger, something philosophical. For me, it *is* a good time. Beanie Upsell steps out in a glimmer of the spotlight, kind of thing. Beanie Upsell has her moment at The Ammonite, at the ultimate London nightclub.

I can sense that Ossian is turning some kind of screw. It's in contrast to my first impression of him as slightly detached, with his languid, slightly defiant expression. At some deep level, I feel he's determined to seal some kind of deal. He flicks open a sleek space-grey laptop and starts showing me the website of The Green Ground in Chelsea. It's stylish and elegant and it's got a spa, which is described as 'the ultimate urban sanctuary'. In fact, I'd like to spend a whole day just in the spa, the chlorine-free pool, the steam room, and have treatments such as the hot stone therapy.

I'm glad Juliet's not here, because she'd say there's not just a red light flashing but a fireball exploding. I think at this moment I do at least see a red light – perhaps a more mundane one, though, like a red traffic light.

"But why me?" I ask again. "You could ask anyone."

"Because… because it's a big thing to face alone; and I'm assuming you want to… as much as I do."

Ossian touches my hand.

"Of course, I'd love to. I hate going to parties on my

own, too. I'm really looking forward to it."

I ask Ossian if I can borrow a couple of items from the 'ex's' drawer', because I don't have anything suitable for a party at The Ammonite and he lets me empty the whole coffer of treasure and sift through it. I snaffle a paint-print Carven mini skirt, an Isabel Marant Etoile T-shirt and cardigan, and of course I take away the clothes I'm already wearing, the Izzy Lane jumper and the sparkly velour leggings. I don't have any snazzy jacket or shoes at home – or a bag for that matter – but I don't want to appear greedy and ask him if he's got any stashed somewhere else. I quickly assess my existing luggage situation: all I've got is a black nylon sports bag with a 'Sony' logo on the side and a large orange and yellow hessian bag that I found abandoned in the courtyard of the first ever flat I rented. I'd given it a good wash and used it as a mainstay for the odd trip. But I don't think it's going to be up to scratch for The Green Ground in Chelsea.

By 9pm, I insist that I have to get back home.

"You can't put those on, they're completely soaked!" Ossian remonstrates, as I attempt to put on my wet shoes and jacket. "Come here a minute. I've got a solution."

I follow Ossian into the spare room and he opens the wardrobe. "These were left behind by Naomi. She was about your size."

Hanging on a rail are a black cotton blazer and a cropped velvet jacket. I check the blazer's label – People Tree.

"This is organic cotton! I don't suppose I could borrow it."

"Take it!" says Ossian. "Keep it!"

"What if Naomi rings you up and wants to come and collect her things?"

"The last thing she said was that she didn't want to see me ever again. Anyway, she threw all my clothes out of the window of her London flat and by the time I went to get them, someone had either helped themselves or they'd gone in a rubbish cart. So, at least I've treated these resources with a little more respect. Keep it! Have both of them!"

"It's too much. I'll just take the People Tree one for now."

I end up trying on some Oliveira shoes with a diamanté strap and some Kaveri vegan ankle boots.

"These actually fit me! These are vegan shoes, too!"

"Oh, those were definitely Naomi's then. She was a vegan."

"*Was* a vegan? Is she still a vegan?"

"Not any more. No."

"Why did you break up?"

"Oh, you know, the usual. Life goes wrong… Take a bag, you'll need something to carry the clothes in."

"Hey, there isn't any chance Naomi is going to be at this party? I mean, I'd die if she saw me there wearing her clothes."

"No. There's no chance Naomi is going to be there."

I'm about to ask him if Naomi knows Honey Gardener, but Ossian's jaw looks clenched.

He slings a weekend travel bag out of the wardrobe; the kind of bag that I probably couldn't find even if I tried. In pinks and reds, it looks like it's made from antique Kilim carpet.

By some process of osmosis, I'm beginning to feel dependent on present luxuries, and the promise of more luxury to come: sleek urban spaces with subtle lighting, modern alchemy, turquoise spa pools – and the anticipation of mixing with artistic types at The Ammonite, and drinking chic cocktails with an innovative twist.

2 6

Candy Box Crush

It's dark so Ossian wants to give me a lift, but I persuade him I need some fresh air after my day in the office. It's stopped raining and a pleasant, cool wind blows through my hair as I walk on the pavement at the side of the twisting road down to the seafront. My new antique Kilim bag, full of designer booty, is looped over my arm.

The wind is blowing the remaining clouds across the night sky and the moon, which still looks full and completely round, shines on the calm sea. Despite the light pollution nearer the shore, a few pinpricks of stars are visible. I think back to the one place I experienced the sky as a starry dome, at a hill farm in Provence. It was a glimpse of what ancient people might have experienced all the time. I try to recall the perception I had back then: that we lived on one planet among many, a sense of the universe that made me feel completely free. It's just a memory now; a memory of a memory. As I continue down the winding road, I vow to myself that

I'll try to be somewhere I can experience it again. It's not an experience that can be bought. It was an experience stumbled upon by my 18-year-old self, on my journey to learn about organic gardening, to 'save the planet', but perhaps it was the perception of planets, the cosmos, that saved me. Or does that perception make things more difficult? Afterwards, you can never settle totally for the man-made version of events. But it's not a perception you can, or want to, undo.

At some level I must have changed, not only because my plans for a life of organic gardening sailed into the sunset and disappeared, but because now I feel some hunger for the manufactured luxury of spa pools and the glamour of a moment in the spotlight, or, hopefully, even a chance of something more permanent in the film industry. I don't assume I can get into acting – but perhaps I can gradually gain experience on set, learn how to make a short film and have a go at writing a screenplay.

Who have I become, walking down this undulating path to the sea, clutching a designer bag full of designer clothes that belonged to Ossian Brohmer's ex-girlfriend? I reason to myself it's recycling, it's reusing clothes, it's a good thing. And this chance to step into the art world is a good thing too: a chance to break out of a straitjacket, to escape from the confines of grey walls and to say something to the world. Life isn't a series of natural starry domes on a plate, not in the twenty-first century. Perhaps it's a different kind of web in the twenty-first century, like finding a niche in the World Wide Web, rather than a niche in an ecosystem. I long for the ecosystem, but somehow I'm detached, caught up in something else, and what's unfolding over the last few days is the best thing that's happened in the last one and a half decades. It's a kind of freedom in itself. A freedom that could be more lasting, perhaps.

I'm passing Louis's place. I'll have to 'confess' about the weekend trip with Ossian sooner or later, so I press the buzzer.

"Hullo?"

"It's me! It's Beanie!"

The release mechanism fizzes and I enter the lobby.

He opens the inner door to see me standing there in the velour sparkly leggings and the Izzy Lane jumper and the Kilim-carpet bag slung over my shoulder. He whistles – not a wolf whistle, but more an expulsion of air shaped into a whistle.

"Nice threads. Don't tell me Ossian's pimping you up and buying you clothes."

"No, they were left behind by his ex." I march in and plump myself down on his vintage leather sofa. "Or his various exes."

"Classy. Just how many exes has he been through up there in his ramshackle house? He's only lived there for about two years... What's with the overnight bag? Going on a sleepover somewhere, are we?"

"I am, actually. I needed to borrow some clothes because I'm going on this overnight trip. We're going to a birthday party at The Ammonite."

"The Ammonite? What do you mean, you're 'going on a trip'?"

"I'm going away for a night. Yes, me, little old me, getting out into the world. You stand there with your eyebrows raised and your eyes all wide and goggly and your Barcelona tan – yes, your Barcelona tan – implying that I should keep things safe. Boring and safe. Better safe than sorry, etcetera… We went through all this last time… By the way, I don't suppose I could have a cappuccino?"

"You just need to answer one question first, sunshine. Are you in a double room or separate rooms?"

"How should I know?"

"What do you mean, 'How should I know?' Surely that's the first thing you know if you're going on a trip with someone?"

"Well, I'm very sorry but he didn't say. And I didn't ask because I just thought it was churlish to ask, when I'm getting taken to some hot-shot hotel. After all, we slept perfectly platonically in the same bed before. It would be like if you and I went on holiday together and shared a room to save money."

"Beanie, if we ever go on holiday, I'm not sharing a room with you. If I go on holiday as a singleton, I'm going on holiday to get lucky and I don't need you in the bed with me."

"Anyway, the fact is, if some hot male film director invited you on a weekend trip to a film festival, I'm sure you'd go."

"What about Simon?"

"Not that chestnut again. I'll be back by Sunday at the latest and Simon isn't even back in the country for another two weeks."

"Well, that doesn't bode well."

"What?"

"Calling Simon a chestnut."

"You know what I mean… The nature of reality is full of dualities and I've decided that in order to live a happy and successful life I need to learn how to juggle and resolve dualities, rather than think everything is one choice over another."

Louis sighs. He's standing there, just standing there, with his hands on his hips. He's looking quite dapper. For some reason, his hair still has this new, ruffled look that incorporates a 'natural' quiff.

"Can I please now have one of your delicious cappuccinos?"

"It's 9.30 at night... a bit late for coffee." He runs a hand through his new hairstyle.

"It's just, I haven't had a coffee all day. All they had at the police station was Bird's Mellow. Anyway how's your love life? You're looking quite dapper with that retro-but-on-trend hairstyle, and your skin has this kind of buffed, shiny look."

He actually blushes, looks sheepish, and the shiny, resilient demeanour crumples, like some plug has been pulled.

"Okay. I admit it. I've got my eye on someone called Rupert."

"Woo! Why didn't you tell me?"

"It's early days. It's like a seed in the dark. It's best hidden, not yanked into the cold light of day."

"Wow, you're seeing him *secretly*?"

"No. In fact, I'm not even sure if he's particularly aware of my existence."

"How can you hope to… you know… if he doesn't even know you exist?"

"Ha, ha, ha. Very funny, Beanie."

Louis's expression still looks like someone popped a taut drum skin with a pin.

"I'm in a bit of a state. I think every guy in town would really like to go out with him... Okay, I'll just go and make some cappuccinos. I kind of need to calm myself down. My breathing goes funny just thinking about him."

Louis goes into the kitchen and I do something I shouldn't. I go over to the shelf of DVDs and take out *The Index of Dreams*. Bingo. The little bag of pills is still there. For a moment, I pretend just to be looking at the DVD cover, just to get into the role of an innocent person reading a DVD cover, and then I ease out the bag from its hiding place. If Louis comes in, I'll just be like, "Hey! What are these doing here?" The problem is, there are only three left. Three... two? It's all the same, really, when it comes to a pill that you take, when you've possibly already had a couple of drinks, ready to go out for the night. Three... two? Who's to remember?

I slip one out of the bag.

Damn, the leggings have no pockets, so I just hold it in my fist until I can get back to my bag, which is inside the antique carpet bag. I click it open and zip it into a tiny pocket, safe and sound. I sprawl back on the leather sofa, pick up a copy of *Attitude*, and immerse myself in a boring article about One Direction.

He brings through a tray with the cappuccinos and some

fancy, wafer-thin biscuits with a taut anticipation in his movements, like a suspect struggling with a burden of information, a suspect who, although nervous, can't wait to confess.

"This is going to keep me awake all night. I'll be lying there, tortured, awake for hours, thinking about Rupert."

He brings over his laptop and puts it on the coffee table so we can both see the screen, and – for a moment I think his hand is actually shaking slightly – taps in the name 'Rupert Khan'.

"*This*... is Rupert."

"Oh! It's Roo!"

There's a photo of Roo standing in his photographic studio. Black and white photos are pinned to the walls. The ones in view show people – the kind of people in town that I don't look at too closely, people who look a bit weather-beaten from drugs, people who I feel afraid of usually, except perhaps when I was dancing at Chambre Magique, when I felt connected. Roo's violet blue eyes stand out in his dark, classically handsome face.

"What do you mean 'Roo'?"

"It's Roo! I met him yesterday. On location with Ossian. He came up to London with us. Took photos on location."

"For fuck's sake. Ossian Brohmer! He has to get his finger in every pie! Well if you already know all about 'Roo', then you don't need me to explain who he is." Louis snaps the lid of his laptop back down.

"Hey! Wait! Let me see! Don't be cross! It's not *my fault* that Ossian asked him to come up to London!"

Photographer Chooses Difficult Subjects
St Martin's Art School graduate Rupert Khan has recently
landed in increasingly up-and-coming Quinton-on-Sea,
which is attracting artists, beatniks and others both disenfran-
chised and disillusioned by the spiralling costs of the capital.
I caught up with Rupert at his photographic studio, which
he has set up in the basement of The Old Chocolate Factory.

Do you find Quinton-on-Sea an inspirational backdrop for
your work?

Basically, I like to focus on the aspects of life which we
see every day, but which we tend to look away from, such
as those living on the edges, those marginalised by frag-
mented social backgrounds. I'm also drawn to the hidden
aspects behind the every day, so you see, here, this is a photo
of East European immigrants queuing at 5am on the sea
front for the buses that take them to the 'chicken-processing'
factory 10 miles away. People see the sanitised chicken in the
supermarket, and they see an idealised picture of a chicken
in a storybook, perhaps in natural surroundings, but they
skip this reality in the middle, whether it's the impact on
humans or the impact on animals. So, to me, a photo has to
be striking, it has to be good in itself, but it's about having
a wider impact...

"He's impossibly, painfully, uber cool without
trying to be," I agree. "He's even more cool because he's
focussed, engaged."

"Not engaged in the romantic sense, I hope."

"Are you sure you can handle an infatuation with
this guy because it's true that practically every man and

woman in this town would be instantaneously attracted to him."

"Well, I can't help it! I can't help myself! At lunchtime I decided to go for a walk past The Old Chocolate Factory. And every time I want to buy a coffee, I go to the cafe that's nearest The Old Chocolate Factory. I can't help myself."

"His ruffled quiff look is quite cool."

Looking sheepish again, Louis begins smoothing his hair back into his usual style.

"Oh, don't change it! It looks quite good! But are you even totally sure he's gay?"

"He must be! I saw him in The Candy Box. Last Friday, when you met up with Simon. He was at The Candy Box. He's got to be!"

Finally, back at home, I'm able to reply to Simon's email. I re-read his earlier message with a twinge of guilt that I've stepped into Ossian Brohmer's world, that he's been usurped, actually, by Ossian's world. It's as though a coil of energy leaps forward from my solar plexus and then springs back with a sense of disappointment. Momentarily, I feel uncertain, discouraged, upset. I'm so tired, I skip my plan to scatter cedarwood oil drops on my pillow and find the perfect words.

Dear Simon

Sorry not to reply straightaway. I've been typing at the local police station! I hope you're having a lovely time. When is your daughter's wedding? It makes me happy to think you'd feel happier if I was there. It would be so lovely to be there with you!

I'm off to a party at The Ammonite this weekend!

Thinking about you too – quite a lot.

Beanie XX

I press 'send', and the email whooshes off. Done.

I need to sort out my outfit for Friday. The paint-print mini skirt, perhaps? I match it with the red jumper, but it might get a bit too hot at a party. Next, I try it on with my dark blue, sequinned halter neck top, and stand on the edge of the bath, trying to glean the overall effect in the mirror. I'm having to crouch over, so I can only view myself one half at a time and imagine the all-inclusive impression. Does the top look a bit trailer-trash with its sequins... or does it look classy? I decide it looks *groovy*. It has just a couple of rows of sequins, after all – something to catch the light, add a bit of sparkle.

I stand up straight to look at the reflection of my lower half. My legs don't look too bad. They're a little more tanned than I thought. Perhaps I could buy some fake tan and smooth it on to top up the colour, just to be on the safe side? It would be handy to have a full-length mirror. My mother offered me an old one about ten years ago, and I'd wondered who on earth would want a full-length mirror? I guess people who have 'events' to go out to, that's who. I wax my legs and try on the whole outfit with my legs bare and the 'suede' effect ankle boots – a combo which I've gleaned from recent fashion pages somewhere or other.

Next I ferret about for the makeup that I bought last week, and put on a tiny bit of the foundation and mascara. I know there's an old pink-tinted lip balm somewhere that I acquired about fifteen years ago when someone invited me to a Cambridge May Ball. I just have to find it in order to finish 'the look'. Half an hour later I'm rummaging through a box of bric-a-brac – old, perished rubber bands, batteries, bits of string, bits of ribbon from birthday and Christmas presents, a pencil sharpener shaped like a ladybird... and finally I detect the small, circular plastic packaging that constitutes the sum total of my makeup (or *did* until I splashed out last week). I add a slick to my lips. It feels a little... congealed? It tastes a little... bitter? I throw it in the bin, along with the perished rubber bands, glad that they're so clearly beyond use that I don't need to prevaricate.

27

The Crest of the Wave

I'm walking to the police station for my second day of transcription and I'm wearing the Isabel Marant printed T-shirt as I simply couldn't wait until Friday to wear something from my new stash. Ossian is on location for the next two days so I don't have to worry about him turning up at Baxters to give me a lift home or anything like that. And I can tell the agency I'm not available next week, if they ask me back. End of problem. Then I've got a mini-break-with-a-difference to look forward to. I get that feeling again – a feeling that a large breaker is crashing over me, or through me, actually, through my centre. It's the strangeness of being suddenly swept up in something so completely different and being strong enough to take it in my stride.

I've even taken the time to pack a decent, healthy lunch: organic salad leaves, cherry tomatoes and cucumber with a delicious garlicky dressing, a chunk of sourdough bread, nuts and a carob bar. The sun reflects on the sea's wavelets, like thousands of sparkling diamonds, as I make my way along the promenade. The air is sparky, autumnal, that blend of warmth and cool that presages an Indian summer. I feel glad to be alive. It'd be cool to not be working today... but still, just three more days.

The others are already at their workstations, tap-tapping away, looking like they've been in situ for hours. As I walk in, I'm sure one of the girls gives the girl seated to her right, near the window, a 'knowing look'.

"Good morning, Sabina!"

Was that a straightforward 'good morning' or was it a sarcastic 'Morning... hope I'm not keeping you up, kind of 'morning'?'

"Am I late?" I ask, knowing full well it's already seven minutes past 9am.

"No, not at all. Some of us start at half eight. Flexi time."

The day passes pleasantly enough, much like the day before, really, except the sun is shining. At lunchtime I walk down to the seafront and eat my healthy packed lunch sitting on the pebbles, with a sense of relief to be away from people. I don't want to interact with the secretaries today. It's actually kind of a relief that I won't be seeing Ossian till Friday. I'd rather not even see Louis right now, with his bossy protestations about me and his neurosis about Rupert. I mean, I'd love to hear all the gossip about Rupert, but not right this second. It's not likely I'll run into Louis anyway as he'll be spending his lunch hour scouring all the coffee shops near The Old Chocolate Factory. I close my eyes and just enjoy the golden September sun.

At 1.45pm, I nip over the road to the health food

shop and treat myself to an organic lip balm gloss that will, apparently, leave a 'berry like' translucent colour on my lips with a 'moderate glow'. As soon as I've paid for it, I run the balm over my lips, and think how nice it would be to keep working on my makeover, rather than re-enter the typing pool with its work bays and plastic, pleated blinds to block out the sun. I'm not even sure why I signed up for temping in the first place. I'm Beanie Upsell, who doesn't look like a secretary, who *isn't* a secretary, who could step out onto the crest of a wave, I tell myself.

I'm just setting off from the health food shop when, in the distance, by the traffic lights, I think I see Ossian's car. Or a car that's identical to Ossian's, because, of course, Ossian is on location.

28

Witness Statement

It's happening. Or very nearly. It's 4pm on Friday and I'm just transcribing the last interview that I'll be working on today. I listen to the contents thinking how this subject matter – involving a man exposing himself every morning at his front door – this world of petty, sordid crime, is so at odds with the world I'll be stepping into very, very soon. I'm going to be a little bit of an imposter, really, because my world is this office world, invisible, unseen; a world where I listen to secretaries talking about diets and meal replacement formulas and Ann Summers parties. For the last three days, I've been more withdrawn, keeping my secret to myself – and feeling sartorially and ethically superior in my Izzy Lane jumper.

I transcribe the last part of the interview where the detective inspector asks the suspect if he would like to add anything. "No, not really," says the man. "I'll switch the recording device off now. This interview is concluded at 14.12 hours," says the DI.

I save the document and go to the case-list to mark it as complete. Suddenly, I remember that I haven't packed a swimming costume in my weekender bag. I'll need a swimming costume for the spa. I make a mental note to do this as part of my 15-minute action plan as soon as I get home – my 15-minute action plan before Ossian comes to collect me from The Promenade in his dinky racing green car.

- Find swimming costume

- Shower

- Get dressed

- Make-up

"No point starting anything new," says Maureen, passing my desk. "Nearly home time."

"I've got 10 minutes left. Why don't I quickly do a short statement?" I saunter over to the pending basket. The statement at the top of the pile is a long one, so I look underneath and pick up the next document, which is only a two-pager.

Right away, somewhere in the midst of the photo-copied, messy, handwritten script, I think I see the words 'Ossian Brohmer'.

"That's very diligent of you! You really don't need to. Just relax." Maureen has just retouched her lipstick. Her ruby lips stretch into a wide, friendly smile and I can see a tiny ruby speck on one of her front teeth.

"Really, it's no problem."

She'll have to physically wrestle it from me if she wants it back, I think, taking it to my desk. I click on the computerised list to show that I've taken the statement marked 'Mayer, Lauren'.

I'm making this statement simply to register my concern. It's not an accusation of any kind. I got to know the film director, Ossian Brohmer, when he came to live in Quinton-on-Sea in January 2013. Our relationship was merely platonic and our friendship revolved around our mutual interest in the arts.

On Saturday 14 February 2015, I attended a Valentine Ball at the Harlequin Hall in Lovington Street. Ossian was also there. When I left at approximately midnight, Ossian Brohmer came back with me to my house at 6 Bixley Place, Quinton-on-Sea and slept in my bed – just in a platonic sense. When I awoke the next day, I couldn't remember anything about my journey home from The Harlequin Hall or inviting Ossian to come back with me. This made me feel quite scared. I wondered if I'd drunk so much that I'd blacked-out, but I know I only consumed three glasses of sparkling wine that evening, which wouldn't be enough to make me black out. I've never lost consciousness from drinking alcohol before. I would say that the maximum I've ever drunk over the course of an evening is ten units, and although that quantity made me feel very drunk, I didn't lose consciousness. I did consider the possibility that someone had spiked my drink, but I certainly didn't suspect Ossian, who was a trusted friend, and decided to put the whole incident behind me.

Later in the year, one day in early July, I was getting my outfit ready for my sister's wedding. I tried on the dress I had bought and went to my jewellery box, which is always kept in a drawer in my bedroom dressing table, to take out the diamond necklace, which I had inherited from my great-grandmother. I was worried to see the diamond necklace was no longer there. I spent two days searching the entire house, but the necklace was missing. The house had been kept secure at all times and at no point during the time I have lived at the house has there been any sign of a break-in. Between January and July, the only people who stayed overnight at my house were Ossian Brohmer (who stayed on just the one occasion on the night of 14-15 February), my sister, and my parents.

I have no domestic staff and nobody else has a key to my house except my sister. I can also add that I know the necklace was still in my possession until at least 1st January 2015, as I wore it for a New Year's Eve party, and I replaced it in the box afterwards.

Also, I would like to add that there have been several social gatherings at my house, although no one went upstairs as the only rooms we used were downstairs, including the down-stairs toilet. Ossian was the only non-family member who had stayed, but I didn't think for a moment he would steal a necklace – and I can't say I particularly suspect him even now.

However, about one week ago, a friend of mine who lives in London, Alison Dewberry, of 2 The Heights, Hilly Lane, SE13, was talking to Simon Bentley of 44 Oxferry Road, N1, who is the brother of Ossian Brohmer's ex-girlfriend, Naomi Bentley (now deceased). Naomi Bentley committed suicide in October 2014. I don't know the exact date. Simon mentioned that he was the Executor of Naomi's estate and that the day before her death, £2,000 cash had been withdrawn from her account, and that there had never been any explanation for where the cash had gone. I can't say the withdrawal of the money was connected to Ossian Brohmer in any way whatsoever.

The reason I am making the statement is that I just want the above-mentioned incidences, of the missing necklace and the missing money, on record, even though I acknowledge that Ossian Brohmer's connection to these incidents could be considered quite tenuous.

There's just one other point I'd like to add, which may or may not be relevant. Simon Bentley also mentioned to Alison Dewberry that although his sister wasn't in a relationship with Ossian Brohmer at the time of her death, she had visited him in the week before she killed herself, and at that time she was already feeling very depressed and vulnerable. Naomi was very keen on animal rights and, allegedly, Ossian Brohmer showed her an animal rights video he had found on the Internet, which was, apparently, the worst case of animal cruelty she'd ever seen. Her brother said that after that visit she seemed different, that she was haunted by the images she had seen and this made her feel suicidal. I acknowledge, however, there is no evidence that Ossian Brohmer is directly connected to her suicide.

Signature: Lauren Mayer

I drop the typed statement in Maureen's 'completed work' basket.

"That was quite a long statement in the end! You certainly finished it at lightning speed. Well…" Maureen looks at her watch, "I'd say that's 4.30 on the dot, now! Doing anything special this weekend?"

"Just keeping it low key, thanks. What about you?"

"Out for a Chinese with the family tonight. Well, Sabina, thanks so much for all your hard work. We're almost up-to-date. We might just want you for one day next week, and then that'll be it. Would you be up for doing one more day, if I let the agency know the updated position on Monday?"

"Sure. No problem!"

"Are you alright, Sabina? You look very pale."

"I'm fine, thank you."

"Get yourself into the fresh air!"

I need to act normal, at least till I get back home. "Act normal," I tell myself, over and over, as I go through the motions of logging off, picking up my bag and saying a cheerful goodbye to Maureen and the secretaries.

I find myself heading towards the lower ground floor, where the cells are located. I've overshot my turning on the stairwell. I climb the stairs, retracing my steps to the ground level and make it through the back door. Outside, even though it's overcast, it feels ridiculously bright in contrast to the dark interior and fluorescent lighting of the police station. I wrap my arms around me, against the wind, as though it could be the spirit of Naomi wrapping her arms around me, in her red cashmere jumper – her jumper that's next to my skin. Or perhaps it's me wanting to put *my* arms around Naomi, protecting her from the world, even though she's not here anymore. Or protecting her from… I don't like to think it… Ossian Brohmer? But, as Lauren Mayer, said, *his connection to the incidents could be considered quite tenuous.*

I can't help but think about some of the animal rights videos I've seen – things that made me want to think 'good riddance' to the planet and everything that goes on. I'd heard of one particular one that I'd avoided seeing. I'd only heard what it was about. But it was enough for images to start flashing in front of me. Images you can never 'unsee'. Suddenly, I hate Ossian Brohmer for sticking his nose into matters that didn't concern him, issues that he didn't concern himself with in any serious way. For meddling with a life.

A light rain begins to fall, and that's when I realise I've left my jacket at the station, on the back of the office chair. I toy with the idea of just leaving it there until Monday – after all, maybe I'm back there on Monday anyway. I reach into my bag to check for my keys. They're not there. Frantically, I check every pocket and inside every zip, but they're not there. They must be in my jacket. I climb back up the hill, towards the police station. By the back door, I key in the combination code and go in. Breathlessly, sweating, I go back up to the first floor, to the office, and take my jacket. The keys are in the pocket. The clock on the wall shows it's 4.50pm. Ossian will be at The Promenade to pick me up in 25 minutes. I need to run.

I'm sweating so much that I want to take the jumper off, but I can't as I've only got a camisole on underneath. I take the steps two at a time. The quicker the better, before anyone sees me, as I know I look like I've been crying. Ridiculously, I find myself heading to the lower ground floor. I've missed my turning again.

"Are you alright, love?" asks a uniformed WPC.

"Sorry. I've just been temping here. I was looking for the exit."

"Follow me. You'll be out in a jiffy." We come to a reinforced door on the ground floor and she taps in a combination code. The door opens directly into reception.

"There you go, okay."

She closes the door behind me and I head past the reception desk, towards the swing doors of the entrance. I'm actually further away now from my route home, as I've got to walk through the main car park before I get to the pavement.

I'm just at the door, pushing it open, when the receptionist calls out, "Have a nice weekend!"

I turn and look back over my shoulder, "Thank you! And you!" Just at that moment, I glimpse, hunched on an orange plastic chair in the corner of reception, holding a broadsheet newspaper open in front of him, obscuring his face completely, a figure wearing electric blue jeans and a plum floral shirt.

Back home, I look in the bathroom mirror. My eyes are bloodshot, puffy, and my face is completely white. Ossian will be arriving in his Morris Minor in precisely ten minutes. Or will he? What was he doing at the police station? I try to recall the moment I walked through reception. A few seconds. That was all. There was no movement, no sound of anyone suddenly picking up a paper. He was already holding up the paper, obscuring himself, embarrassed, perhaps, to be at the station. He can't have seen me – although I can't be sure. My head spins in a panic. Suddenly, I know that I'm afraid of Ossian Brohmer. The person who I thought would cure me of my fear of life, remove my fear of life, by making oblivion easy. I'm afraid of him.

I find myself unable to move, to get ready – to shower, change or put on make-up. Or to find my swimming costume and add it to the packed bag. Suddenly, the spa doesn't seem particularly important any more. Or desirable. I'm not even sure I can face getting into Ossian's car. Even the idea of going to The Ammonite – of meeting Honey Gardener and Ossian's friends, who may or may not have known Naomi Bentley – makes me feel nauseous. Suddenly, I know with total clarity that even if Ossian isn't connected to 'the incidents' that I need to disassociate from him; that I *want* to disassociate from him.

6 pm. Even though I'm expecting the intercom to buzz any second, I jump when it does. I freeze. I don't get up and press the entrance-door release button. Maybe I could just pretend I'm not here. Maybe I could ring Louis. But then I hear feet on the stairs, marching across the landing. Someone must have left the Yale lock on its catch again. There's a fist rapping on my door. I rationalise quickly. He's not going to *do* anything. Even if he saw me at the police station. He's not going to *do* anything. He's angry. That's all.

I open the door.

He's standing there, in his electric-blue jeans and plum floral shirt, perspiration on his face. He wipes his face with his sleeve.

"We need to talk." His voice is tight, strained.

I stand back for him to come in. He walks in and paces around the room.

"This place is foul. We'll go back to mine. To talk."

"We can talk here."

"No. We'll go to The Pineapple. At least it's got a sea view, for Christ's sake, and a bit of fresh air."

"Okay." I pick up my shoulder bag.

"Where's the weekend bag?"

"We're still going to London?"

"Of course we're still going to London, for Christ's sake. We just need to talk first, that's all. Talk everything over, in a civilised manner, over a cup of tea."

I pick up the Kilim bag and wrap my arms around it, holding it in front of me like reinforcement. I follow Ossian's thumping footsteps down the stairs, looking at the perspiration that's soaked into the back of his shirt.

Outside, I catch the smell of the sea air mixed with the sharp, masculine scent of Ossian's sweat, as he slings my weekender bag in the boot.

"Phew. For a moment, I thought you were going to refuse to come. I was afraid my powers of seduction had really gone off the boil." He slams down the door of the boot, gets into the driving seat and starts the engine.

29

The Falling Tower

We speed along the seafront and I wonder if I've got everything out of proportion. Perhaps some neural pathway has been activated, triggering childhood fears, childhood ghosts. I've always been afraid of something or other, all my life. Just being trapped in an office can bring me out in a cold sweat. I shouldn't *project* my fears onto Ossian. Besides which, by tomorrow night, I'll be free again. I just need to fulfil my social obligations over the next twenty-four hours, negotiate my way through them like a bomb disposal expert and then exit delicately. That's all. Perhaps I should even make the most of it, if these are my last few hours with Ossian. Like a mantra, I repeat over and over, *Ossian Brohmer, famous, successful film director... Ossian Brohmer, famous, successful Director of The Index of Dreams,* in case I'm in danger of forgetting who he is – or at least the person who he *was,* in my eyes, for the last twenty years.

I tell myself that I'm viewing the seafront, at

accelerated speed, from the privileged position of Ossian Brohmer's trendy, vintage car. We stop at a set of traffic lights and I can see a pile of dog poop on the promenade and someone else's dog is squatting down doing another poop on one of the large pink paving stones. I'm beyond it all, beyond the usual day-to-day detritus, I tell myself. The car gathers speed again and we zoom away from the poop and the occasional discarded fast-food polystyrene box, and everything else that I'm used to passing at close quarters, at walking pace.

At the effortless touch of an accelerator, we glide up the winding road, through the old gateposts and into the driveway of The Pineapple.

"When I first bought this place, it was called bloody *Windrush*. Imagine that! It sounded like some bloody English suburban bungalow." Ossian slams on the brakes. "Let's go in."

Gingerly, I follow his fast-paced figure through the Gothic door and into the old gardener's cottage.

"Make yourself a cup of tea. I just need to do something upstairs... freshen up." He strides up the stairs, two at a time.

I admit to myself that, up until this point, I had some latent fear, some half-formed thought that his only plan in bringing me here was to slip rohypnol into my tea. But now here I am making the cup of tea myself. Perhaps I'm overreacting. Perhaps I'm being overly dramatic.

As I sip the hot tea, I stare at Ossian's photos of glamorous girlfriends in glamorous locations, pinned on the corkboard, wondering if any of them is Naomi. I study the breezy, carefree expression of the girl in the wicker chair, on the patio in what looks like Tuscany, a burst of azure morning glories around her head. Even though I'm about to go on a 'dream trip' with Ossian Brohmer, I'm the dog who's about to have its day, this photo of happiness, the spontaneous smile of this beautiful woman, makes me feel regret – regret for the shadow that is already cast; cast before the party – the ultimate party at The Ammonite – is even started. It's back to square one. A too familiar feeling of confusion and reversal shoots back and forth inside me – a reversal of hope, a beautiful tower crashing down. I'm a fool for thinking I could have a different kind of life.

I stare through the Gothic window at the line of ash, with the defoliated ends of the branches waving like skeletal arms. Though the window is Gothic, this isn't some Gothic drama, I tell myself. It's just the story of my life, of Beanie Upsell returning to her normal baseline. And upstairs is some film director who hasn't been able to get anything off the ground for the last twenty years, who's probably, right this second, snorting a line of cocaine or whatever it is that's sent him hurtling upstairs. And I haven't got the guts to tell him to piss off, basically. I'm going to go through this charade of going to the party, of staying at the hotel, before I extricate myself. It's low drama; it's not high drama. It's not Gothic horror. Let's face it, I tell myself, Ossian might be a fool but he's not so foolish as to do anything really bad and get himself into real trouble.

30

A Proposal

He comes into the kitchen, looking showered and refreshed, now dressed in violet blue jeans and a pink floral shirt, and claps his hands.

"Ready? By the way, sorry for the way I behaved just now."

"It's okay."

"No. It's not okay. It was totally unacceptable. I just needed to touch base, but I'm absolutely fine now. But, yeah… I guess I'm still a bit freaked out…" Ossian looks down, as though he's cogitating. Then his face changes, transforms into a mask, the mask of a ghoul. Ugly. He looks up again, straight at me. "I just need to know what the fuck you were doing at the police station just now… suddenly bursting out of some reinforced door, some inner sanctum, at the fucking police station!"

"You saw me at the police station?"

"Don't fucking try and deny it…"

"I didn't think you'd seen me, that's all."

"Well, wouldn't that have been convenient! I looked up at the fucking CCTV screen in the corner of the room, yeah, up high on the wall, and I see fucking Beanie Upsell, in smudgy, grainy, black-and-white, caught on camera, like a fucking criminal, sneaking out the fucking police station… and then a voice, sounding just like Beanie's: "*You too! Have a nice weekend!*" He repeats in a mocking, derogatory tone, "*Have a nice weekend!*""

"I'm sorry. I'm really sorry I didn't tell you… I just happened to be temping there for four days. Out of my whole life, that's the only four days I've ever been at a police station… and, you know, I had the impression you didn't like the police, so I just didn't mention it."

Ossian stares at me. His eyes belong to a madman. "You just didn't mention it? You fucking lied. Told me you were at fucking Baxters. Had me turn up outside Baxters to give you a fucking lift. Christ! You walk around wide-eyed, like some boring, straightforward person who wouldn't say boo to a goose, but actually you're a conniving little shit, Beanie. I need to know what you were doing at the police station. *Exactly* what you were doing, what role you were playing, basically."

"Just typing. That's all."

"Right. I need to ask you a question. What do you know? What did you get to know?"

"I signed the Official Secrets Act. It's all secret. But it's fair to say it was run-of-the-mill. Speeding… drink-driving… shoplifting. The usual stuff. I think I'm allowed to say that much."

He plants his hands on the wall, either side of my shoulders. He leans forward until his ghoul-mask face is within an inch of my own.

"So why aren't you fucking asking what *I* was doing there?"

"That's none of my business."

I stare down at the kitchen's cracked lino, unable to hold his madman's gaze. I'm absorbing the appearance of the lino in minute detail, the way it has a light-blue marbled effect, the way the edge is an inch short of the units. Whoever laid it must have measured it incorrectly. So for forty years, or whatever, there's been a gap there, where all the dust and dirt gathers, and probably sticks slightly, even when you try and clean it.

I wonder if it's me. Whether there's something in me that brings out the worst in people. Even Naomi, or whoever it is in the photo, went on holiday with him. They must have got on well enough to go away together – relaxed enough to smile spontaneously on a terrace in Tuscany, relaxed enough to stand the other side of the world, somewhere sunny, your hair tossed around in the wind...

"Why don't I just go home?" My voice sounds tight, strangulated.

He moves abruptly away, walks to the window and stares out, his back to me now, his hands on his hips.

"Home? We've got a plan and I'd like you to stick to it."

"There's no point. I feel like crap. You're angry. I'm sorry, Ossian, but there's no way I'm getting in that car now. I told a white lie, that's all."

He swivels round.

"Are the police aware that you go around telling lies about where you're working? Personally, I think it's a crime."

I don't know what's what any more. Suddenly I'm scared I've done something really wrong. Breached the Official Secrets Act or something. I could end up in prison or something.

Ossian claps his hands.

"Where's my tea? I could really do with a cup of tea. You didn't make me one?"

Suddenly, the rage-mask has dropped and it's his normal Ossian-face again, as though someone pulled a plug and a torrent of tension drained away. His body looks loose, relaxed as he holds the kettle under the tap and fills it with water.

"Another cup?" he asks casually. "Sorry, Beanie, if I freaked you out there. It's just I'm someone who likes to clear the air. Now we've got that little bugbear out of the way, there's something I want to ask you."

He has his back to me, takes something out of his pocket and then turns around. His hands are cupped together, as though there's a tiny creature inside that might escape or, bizarrely, it reminds me of an advertisement I once saw – where the man unclasped his hand to reveal a blue velvet ring box.

"Some people are honest and straightforward and just come out with the truth of what they want to say. For example, they'll say, 'Do you want to be my fuck buddy?' Don't worry, Beanie, that's not what I'm asking you. What I'm asking you is rather more special and unique."

There's a long pause. He takes a deep breath and pauses momentarily again, as though what he has to say is so momentous that it's a bit of a struggle. For one bizarre moment, I do actually wonder whether he *is* about to ask me to marry him.

"What I want to say, Beanie, is this…"

He lifts the 'lid' of his hand to reveal a dozen lozenge-shaped tablets.

"…Will you be my suicide buddy?"

I stare at the white and green lozenges in Ossian Brohmer's hand.

He registers the look on my face. "Don't worry. I know it's a big thing to ask. Just take your time. In fact, why don't I just make us some fresh cups of tea? We can make this our own *Index of Dreams*. It takes time: to discuss feelings about death, to have a party of some kind first, all that kind of thing."

For the first time in my life, I find myself stuttering. "I th-thought we were going to H-Honey Gardener's party. Actually, if you don't mind, I think I'll just go home for a bit. It's quite a big thing to think about."

"That's right, Beanie. It *is* quite a big thing."

"I mean, you could go ahead to Honey Gardener's party and I'll just chill out at home and think about it."

I take a sip of my cold tea. "In fact, I think you'd be happier going on your own to Honey Gardener's. I mean, you need time to think about it, too."

"Don't start me off again, Beanie." With slow deliberation, Ossian places the pills on the kitchen table, then leans over me and puts his hands on my shoulders. His thumbs dig into my flesh with circular movements, as though he's about to give me a neck massage. Then the little movements stop and his thumbs are at the base of my throat. "I don't like being second-guessed. I don't like being told what makes me happy or what I need to do."

His thumbs exert a soupçon of pressure, for emphasis, before he pulls away.

"Now, where's that teapot. You just made tea for one? Not a pot?"

Through the Gothic window, in the distance, I can see a man in a fluorescent vest taking photographs of the ash trees. It feels like another bomb alert. Another bomb that could go off inside Ossian Brohmer any second. I wonder if I could run out of the cottage, out of The Pineapple, and start screaming, "Help! Help!" at the man in the fluorescent vest. But then the man disappears behind the windbreak. I just need to treat everything lightly, play along, *manipulate* Ossian without him being aware of it, I tell myself.

While Ossian busies himself with the teapot and pours out two mugs of tea, I watch as carefully as I can to check he doesn't add any date rape drug or something. He passes me a mug that has the words, "World's Best Dad" emblazoned across it.

"Have you got kids?"

"Don't try to change the subject, Beanie. I'm not talking about kids right now. This is about us. For God's sake, sit down. Relax. We've got all the time in the world."

I sit down and Ossian sits himself in a wooden wheel-backed chair at the head of the table. A deep furrow appears between his eyes and, distractedly, he rolls one of the green and white capsules back and forth with his index finger. Rolls it this way and that. Then he divides the pile and makes two neat rows. He leans forward, looking earnestly into my eyes.

"The thing is Beanie, when I met you, I knew you

were *the one*. When you told me you'd waited twenty years to see *The Index of Dreams*, I had this instinct. I *knew* you could be the one."

He stretches his arms and then rolls his head from side to side, as if easing a crick.

"The thing is, Beanie, we could go out on a high. I know I've kind of sprung this on you. The reason is, time is of the essence. I want to go out on a high – for *us* to go out on a high, together. Not desperate, alone, but together – a death pact, united in death. Don't you see? It's more romantic. So, it's not a question of going back home and thinking about it. But about having a party here. Now. We could get ourselves into a really amazing state – I've got everything we could possibly need here – and then we go out seamlessly, on a wave of oblivion. I've even got a gun, if we want it. But I don't think we'll need it. We'll just have a load of feel-good stuff, followed by my special barbiturates from Mexico. Just think, Beanie, you'll never have to go and work in an office ever again. Never have to worry about money or relationships ever again. Or about global warming or any of those things. Or about getting old and ending up in an old people's home."

"But what about your film? I thought you were about to make *The Warehouse*. This could be the film that resurrects you. From the bit I saw, I genuinely thought it was good. I think you should at least make another film first, rather than going out feeling defeated."

"Who the fuck said I was feeling 'defeated'? Who said that? Did anyone say that to you?"

"No! I mean... I just think you could make your film first, and then have a re-think."

"You know what that is, Beanie? A classic example of displacement of your latent death wish. An avoidance technique. False optimism. I haven't even finished the fucking script, Beanie. I've got twenty fucking pages of a script and no fucking money to make a film. That's the truth."

"I'll help you finish the script! I can help you! I *want* to help you! You need to increase the prices on your crowd-funding page. I'm sure there are people who would pay a thousand pounds to have a small part in *The Warehouse!*"

Suddenly Ossian slumps and lays his head on the table.

"I just don't want to try any more. I can't be bothered any more… I've spent all the crowd-funding money on fucking smack. Don't argue with me, Beanie. You're just little innocent Beanie who doesn't even know what it is to crave a whiskey."

I run through my head the idea that I could die in the next few hours and whether it does, in fact, have any appeal. The thought of Simon makes my stomach lurch with longing – and sadness that now, more than ever, I've proved myself unsuitable – here I am in the house of a madman, on the brink of a suicide pact, or teetering on the edge of being coerced into it. It must be at least partially my fault. It's a dream come true, in a nightmarish way.

But fuck it. Even if I'm dysfunctional, without a hope relationship-wise, it's not for Ossian Brohmer to decide what happens in my life… whether I get to ring Simon again, speak to him, see him. 'World's Best Dad!' Is Ossian a father? He's had his chances, his holidays, his girlfriends.

Suddenly, I feel sorry for Beanie Upsell, for her sad little life trudging in and out of the office and her uncertainty about sex, about joining the circle of life. Fuck it, I could at least go on holiday. I wonder whether I'm shallow as small things, rather than big, philosophical things spring to mind: that I've saved all my money and haven't been out for nice meals; that I haven't made a Will. If I die intestate, my parents, who are already rich, will inherit everything, rather than animal charities or environmental charities. Not even Louis will get anything. But most of all I think about Simon. Fuck it. I'm sick of trying to delicately manoeuvre myself around Ossian Brohmer.

I pick up my bag and stand up. "I'll be straight with you, Ossian, I'm not into this. Yes, there are plenty of times in the past when I'd have said 'yes', but not right now. Okay? You need to acknowledge that."

Ossian lurches towards me. His hands are around my neck – properly around my neck.

"You know too much, Beanie. I'm sorry. But you know too much. You're staying here until you come to your senses. Until you agree to what you really want deep down inside of you. Rent-a-death. That's what you want. Right now I could tighten my grip. Tighten it and tighten it. But I wouldn't want that. I don't want to die a murderer. I'm Ossian Brohmer, tragic genius, on an upward curve, about to make another brilliant film, struck down in my prime. You are part of my final mise-en-scène, Beanie. Can't you see that? It's not only good for me, it's good for you. You're not just Beanie Upsell, nonentity, you're Beanie Upsell who died in a suicide pact with the famous film director, Ossian Brohmer."

My voice breaks, it sounds shaky. "Can't we just go to Honey Gardener's party first? I thought we were supposed to do something nice first, choose our dream. Otherwise it's not like *The Index of Dreams*."

Ossian releases his grip. "What was I thinking? I've been selfish. We're all packed up and ready to go. I'd lost my train of thought. Right." He picks up his mug of tea and slugs it back in one. "Right. Good idea. Actually, come to think about it, I'd really like to see Honey Gardener and my old friends one last time."

He turns, goes to the sideboard, grabs a bottle of spirits and, with his back to me, pours out two measures. I get the impression that for one moment there's a surreptitious movement, a shuffling motion with his hands.

"One for the road!" he says, passing me one of the shot glasses. I stare at the shot, not moving. Ossian stares at me, keeps staring at me. His eyes bore into me like a gun held to my head. I sip mine slowly, uncertainly, and Ossian knocks his back in one.

31

U-Turn

Even though we've only been in Ossian's cottage for about twenty minutes, when I step outside it feels more like a year since I felt the wind on my face. I contemplate making a run for it, but I remind myself to diffuse the situation, to act calmly. I'll have all the opportunity in the world to escape in London, as soon as we're surrounded by crowds.

Ossian opens the door of the Morris Minor for me to get in. I like the feel of the old leather seats, the old, faded red leather and the slight polish/petrol smell, that reminds me of the interior of my granny's old Mini – or, rather, I would like the feel of this old car interior if I didn't feel clenched inside, like a block of metal; but not really like metal because it's a block of solid fear – total fear, even though I know I can give Ossian the slip in about one and a half hour's time. When we get to the hotel reception, for example, I could freak out. I could start shouting, "HELP! HELP!" Or I could go into a toilet, lock the door and call the police. But the party would be easiest. Just slip out, amongst the crowd. Onto the crowded streets of London and bolt down into a tube station, onto a bus… Get back to Quinton and go straight to Louis's. Call the police.

The Morris Minor climbs up the hill, past the sprawling suburbs.

"I think this is why you feel trapped in Quinton. Because it's like you've got all this sitting on top of you, all this bloody suburbia, before you get to the country-side. You're kind of hemmed in? I wouldn't have chosen to live here if I weren't on top of the cliffs. But you're not going to be at The Promenade that much longer."

"Well, the lease is another five months."

"The lease?" Ossian laughs. "You're coming back with me to The Pineapple tomorrow, aren't you?"

I laugh awkwardly, and then say jauntily, "Sure." Jaunty, I think. Keep it jaunty.

"Do you ever have that feeling that things are almost perfect but not quite?" he asks.

"Yes…"

"There was something I wanted to get out of the way before this weekend, something I had to deal with, but it's not quite resolved yet."

Finally we're up onto the summit of the hill and the road levels out. There are green fields and we pass the occasional oast house. I feel like I'd be quite happy to travel on and on, back to my roots in the West Country and never return down to the bottom of the hill, down to the seafront of Quinton-on-Sea – or to the cliffs and The Pineapple.

We're passing a layby, when Ossian slows the car and pulls into it. He twists the steering wheel round and performs a U-bend in the middle of the road. A car coming from the opposite direction slams on its brakes and blares its horn. The driver starts shouting and shaking his fist.

"Fucking cunt. Can't he see I was just turning around!"

"Why are we turning around? I thought we were going to the party! We'd agreed it! You said you wanted to see Honey Gardener and all your old friends! PLEASE! I would really like to meet all your old friends!"

"Just shut up, Beanie! I've forgotten something, that's all. We're going back to The Pineapple."

He puts his foot down on the accelerator and looks in the rear view mirror.

I look at the speed dial. 60 miles per hour. It's at that moment that I begin to notice something. A wooziness. A feeling of slipping away. I'm still conscious, but suddenly everything feels at one remove. More numb. I start to care less, even though somewhere in my brain I know I should actually be more worried.

"I need to get away from that cunt who's behind us – shaking his bloody fist and shouting!"

Nothing much has changed, I tell myself, looking at the blur of hedges and then suburbia, as we head back. Nothing except the fact it will be harder to run away from Ossian. Despite the wooziness, I imagine leaping out of the car at the next traffic lights. It will be easy. All I need to do then is flag the car behind and start shouting for help.

We pass through two sets of traffic lights, one green and one amber. By the time we're driving through the old gateposts I feel myself beginning to slump and it's just the seat-belt that's holding me up.

3 2

Escape

I open my eyes. The room is fairly dark, lit by just one small lamp on a side-table. In the distance I hear a sound, a whispering, that could be the wind in the trees, or perhaps it's the susurration of the sea. It smells fusty in here. That particular smell of a damp, unused room in a period house. Old carpets. Antiques. Despite the gloom, I see, with blinding illumination, a light that travels backwards in time, to my fourteen-year-old-self who's tunnelled her way through life, always in the dark. And how *The Index of Dreams* was just the cipher for this feeling, the embodiment, the solution, for a bud that couldn't open.

I'm lying on a settee – an old-fashioned settee. It feels very firm, like a Victorian Chesterfield, and the uphol-stery, with its green Paisley cover, has a large tear. Next to the side-table with the lamp, reclining deep within an armchair, is Ossian. His elbows rest on the chair arms. In one hand he holds a tumbler of whiskey. He stirs and leans forwards, as though roused by my opened eyes. He squints momentarily, then slumps back into the chair.

My limbs feel heavy. I register the thought that, in a way, being drugged makes everything easier. Easier not to panic. Easier to be a victim. All I have to do is be passive and go with the flow. Watch everything happening at one remove. It's not my responsibility any more. Not my responsibility to save myself. To take care of myself. Perhaps, after all, I could have a tête-à-tête with Ossian, make the most of the fact that I'm not alone. Have a glass of good-quality wine. Dabble with some drugs together and then sail away. Sail away into infinity with Ossian Brohmer. Despite his insane behaviour, I can think of worse ways to die. I recall the way he held me as we lay in bed together, that day after Chambre Magique, and think maybe we could 'make up' and lie in each other's arms.

My hand is resting on something that feels silky. Something satiny, unfamiliar on my skin. The sensation jolts me, cuts into my slumbering reverie. I'm wearing something strange. A dress. I run my hand across the material. The silky material comes just to the knee. I can see my clothes, or rather Naomi's clothes – the clothes I was wearing earlier, the velour sparkly leggings and the red cashmere – in a heap at the foot of the settee. What the fuck? Ossian Brohmer is just *too* weird. Too weird. And there are shoes wedged onto my feet. Shoes that are too tight. High-heeled shoes. Like Cinderella shoes. I nudge the shoes, one after the other, against the settee's arm until they fall off.

"Sleeping beauty. You've woken up at last." His tone is diffident.

There's something around my neck. A necklace. Crystals. My hands fumble, searching the back of my neck for the catch and, determined, eventually I undo it.

"It was really fiddly putting that necklace on," he remarks.

In my hands I hold crystals that sparkle even in the gloom. Diamonds.

"I hate diamonds," I say. My voice sounds hoarse, a little groggy. "Or, rather, I hate the *fuss* about diamonds."

I lay the necklace carefully on the floor. After all, Ossian doesn't own this necklace, I'm pretty sure about that.

"And I'd like to put my clothes back on."

"Naomi's clothes."

"Why did you put this dress on me?"

"To go to the party, of course. Had a change of heart. Thought we could pop up to The Ammonite." His voice sounds tired; a little slurred.

I look at the carriage clock on the mantelpiece, but I can't make out where the hands are. There's no sound of ticking anyway. It's as dead as a dodo. As if Ossian Brohmer would bother to keep his carriage clock wound up…

"Bit late now, I guess," slurs Ossian. "…about 1am… Shall I put some music on? How about some music? I'm not in the mood for anything too rocky. Something soft would be better…" He hoists himself out of the armchair and goes over to a sideboard where a piece of slim-line technology sits like a tiny UFO. At the touch of a button, a CD tray smoothly presents itself. Ossian inserts a disk and the machine calmly slides the tray back in.

As soon as the familiar sweet, melancholy piano

music hits me, I enter the other world again. The world of *The Index of Dreams*. A world of emotion. Although it feels a little sadder now. My eyes fill with tears. I feel washed up on a shore.

"You look beautiful," he says as he walks towards me. "Why don't we just lie together for a while? We can make everything feel safe."

Despite everything that happened earlier, there's a wavelength within Ossian Brohmer that locks into a receptor within me; although something does feel different now. Through the fug, I feel a pinprick of regret. Somewhere in the other world out there is Louis… is *Simon*. And now it's the other world that seems to have colour. And here, in Ossian's sitting-room it feels airless, dark. A darkness of bruises, bruised emotion, abuse.

Too drugged to move, I try to make the most of what's on offer. Ossian Brohmer enfolding me in his arms, like the afternoon after we'd been swimming. I rest my head on his chest, on his floral shirt, and feel myself drifting away.

It stirs me awake. A vibrating buzz in the pocket of Ossian's jeans.

"Is that your phone?" I murmur.

"I'll leave it," says Ossian.

I sink back into our reverie. A few moments later, I think I hear something discordant jarring with the music. Perhaps it's something deliberate, a layer of repetitive atonality. But it keeps going and going, insistent.

"Is that your landline?"

"Fuck it. I'll leave it. Let's stay like this for now, because we've got a big decision to make soon."

"Maybe you should answer it?"

There's a click, and then a voice on loud-speaker as the answer machine kicks in. A woman's voice. Loud, slurred, sailing over the melancholy piano notes.

"Ozz! Ozz! It's Honey! Where are you? I was *so* counting on you coming tonight! Pick up the phone! For Christ's sake, pick up the phone! Maybe you have a new girlfriend… maybe you're not even there. I'm making a fool of myself, I know. I just thought… after Naomi… Christ knows, we're *all* still getting over it… but life doesn't go on forever… and I just wanted to say… let's just *do* something… *do* something with our lives, right? We could have a kid together… make a film together. It's not right what people are saying about you… about Naomi… about your one film twenty years ago, about you being finished, laughing about your Golden Raspberry or whatever they called it…"

Abruptly, Ossian disentangles himself from our embrace, gets up, and marches over to the phone.

"For fuck's sake, Honey! Look, I'm sorry I didn't make it to the party, but things aren't great right now. Okay… Okay… Well, maybe… yes, I was asleep… No, I don't have a new girlfriend…"

He's standing there, his back to me. His tall frame in his floral shirt and violet blue jeans. I sit up and realise I have more control of my limbs now. Less grogginess. Less numb. Less at one remove. But with a headache. A bad headache. I get up and tiptoe to the door. Maybe

I'm just going to the kitchen, or to his medicine cabinet, to try and find an aspirin. Or maybe I'm just going to the bathroom to go to the loo.

"… no, no… and what the fuck do you mean? What were people at the party saying about me? Who? Who said that? I'd like to know who said that…"

Then his floral-shirted frame disappears altogether, engulfed in an egg-shaped swivel chair.

"…That's totally insulting. Of course I'm making a new film, Honey! … Yes, I'm absolutely fine, thanks very much… On the edge? Who said that?"

And that's when I slip quietly out of the room, under cover of the music from *The Index of Dreams*.

"…Oh, yes, yes, sorry, I completely forgot. Happy Birthday! How was it? Great! That's really great! Yes, of course I wish I'd come… But *who* said I was on the edge?…."

The voice recedes as I slink into the flagstone hallway and then disappears altogether as I close the Gothic front door behind me.

Outside. Cool night air sharpens my senses; cold sea mist on my face. My life back in my hands. To unfurl. To have another go. To see if I can make it without Ossian Brohmer and *The Index of Dreams*. Start from scratch. Something new.

I don't know whether to run towards the carved steps down to the beach or take the winding road. I picture myself disappearing down the stone staircase, engulfed by night and nature, away from streetlamps and the possibility of a passing Morris Minor.

The moonlight is twinkling and bouncing on the distant wavelets like a pointillist painting as my bare feet carry me swiftly across the dewy, unkempt grass. Despite the danger and the fear, I feel release as I run, away from The Pineapple, away from Ossian Brohmer. I recall the cover of *The Web of Evil* in all its Technicolor glory, with the woman in flight, poised, like an elegant mannequin, looking back, dressed in her off-the-shoulder gown. I don't look over my shoulder. I look ahead, breathing hard, skin sweating, my heart beating; my face tight with dried tears.

I'm half way down the carved steps when it's obvious. The dark vortex below. High tide. Deep. Eddying. Churning. The waves pull back, dragging pebbles in their wake and then surge forward again, smacking the cliffs, rebounding back on themselves.

Reverting to Plan B, I turn and start running back up the stairway. I tell myself to slow down, to save my breath for the more exposed part of the route, but somehow I can't seem to stop myself from hurrying. I'm very nearly at the top when I see him. Standing at the summit of the steps, about ten feet away from me. Ghost-like in the moonlight. He's standing there, stock still, not saying anything. A stance with his legs slightly apart, hands on hips. For a moment, I can't seem to move. I can't seem to do anything. The moonlight casts a shadow on his face, obscuring it.

I run back down the stone staircase. On the bottom step I pause. The waves splosh around my feet. Reaching to the back of my neck, I unzip the dress, step out of it and wade into the black sea. I'm knocked off my feet by a velocity that is indifferent. A gravitational speed. The moon. Nature against me. A primordial force. Salt water stings my eyes, crashes over my head. I'm knocked against rocks, grazed, hurt, and then carried out. An undertow? A riptide? More rocks. Hard knocks. Then a depth with no rocks. Just the occasional silky tangle of seaweed brushing my legs. At moments, I'm pulled under and that's when I know it's all over. Alone, churned in black, briny water. Fathomless. Memories race across my mind. Nearly drowning when I was four years old. I didn't feel afraid. No reaction at all. Underwater in a lily pond. Pulled out by my brother. How the neighbour put me in a dressing gown, on a red velvet stool in front of their sitting-room fire, waiting for my mother to come and collect me. And the first time I wondered down the cul-de-sac on my own. Three years old. An adventurer. An explorer.

I begin to feel like I'm sinking. For a split second, I picture myself in Ossian's company. Imagine how I might have placated him. Drunk with him. Got into an amazing state with him and departed safely anaesthetised on the safety of dry land.

A force pushes me back up and I gulp for air, but take in sea water too. It's impossible to aim for any direction. For what seems like an eternity, the force alternates between pulling me down and delivering me back to the top. Exhausted, I just want it to be over, either way. Of its own volition, my mouth gulps air in the moments on breaking the surface. I'm pushed by more waves, now at a right angle to the shore, rather than further out.

Then the mad tossing eases. The force is spent and my head's above water. The current has carried me in the direction of the harbour. Ancient, within sight. A wall. A rope on an iron ring. Steps, even. I do breast strokes that leave me where I am. The equivalent of running on a running machine, making no progress. But then a gentle surge carries me inland and I swim with it, towards the steps in the seaweed-coated wall.

On jelly legs, I stumble up the steps of slippery algae. I collapse on the moonlit quay, a piece of flotsam. Bruised, bleeding, cold; naked, except for my knickers and camisole. I still feel a sense of threat and my lungs hurt. It hurts when I breathe. But my body keeps breathing.

Unable to move, I wonder if I'll be here till dawn, or whether a late night reveller will find me. I lie curled, gasping, replacing the deficit of oxygen, for what seems like an hour.

In the stillness of the night, I imagine hearing a car engine starting up – a cranky, vintage engine – followed by the sound of tyres crunching on gravel, the sound of the rolling engine getting nearer, in pursuit, the beam of headlights. But no car comes. I force myself onto my feet and start walking, then break into a run and keep running.

I'm almost at Louis's door. I can see car headlights coming towards me... but it's a smooth, modern engine.

Gasping, breathless, I press the buzzer. I've no idea what time it is. I wait and wait. I press again. Nothing. Another car's coming, something with a throaty engine from the headland, from the east. I should have flagged down the zippy modern car. Desperate, I push on the buzzer and leave it there, making its ugly electronic buzz in the middle of the night. Finally, the buzz is cut dead by the abrupt lifting of the receiver.

"Who the fuck is that?"

I gulp. A strange, small, short cry comes out of me.

"What the fuck is going on?"

"Louis! It's me! It's Beanie!"

"Beanie? What the fuck!"

"I've run away. I had to escape. Ossian Brohmer…"

"Beanie? You sound really fucked up. But the thing is, Rupe's here. This is actually the most important night of my entire life. You'll have to get a taxi home…"

"Ossian Brohmer… he wanted me to kill myself…"

The release fizzes and I push the door open.

33

A Non-Suspicious Death

Ossian Brohmer dead at 55

Ossian Brohmer has been found dead at his cliff-top home in Quinton-on-Sea in the early hours of this morning.

The film director's body was discovered by police officers after the alarm was raised by a 35-year-old woman. The woman, said to be living locally, is helping the police with their enquiries.

Two officers attending the scene were forced to break into the cliff-top home after being unable to open the front door.

Kent Police have confirmed: "Police were given cause to attend at an address in Quinton-on-Sea earlier today.

We can confirm that a 55-year-old man was pronounced dead at the scene by South East Coast Ambulance Service. They are now working to establish the circumstances surrounding the death, which is not being treated as suspicious."

The Swedish film director found fame with his 1994 award-winning film *The Index of Dreams*, which chronicled the lives of a group of suicidal teenagers. The film, famously censored for 20 years, was set to enjoy a renaissance with the ban due to be lifted imminently.

The film director's death will come as something of a shock to those who, just earlier in the week, were on location with Brohmer filming his latest feature *The Warehouse* – described on the deceased's Twitter page as 'nordic noir comes to British shores'.

Oscar-winning director Martin Abse described Brohmer's death as "A tragic loss to the film-making community. After an absence of many years, Ossian Brohmer had rekindled his creative flame and was on the cusp of new beginnings. Fans around the world will be shocked and saddened by the director's sudden and premature death."

34

Post Mortem

"Phew! Bad news travels fast! Or maybe I should call it good news? And what bollocks! What absolute bollocks! Though look at that photo of you – it's quite good." Louis points to the image beneath the article and its caption: *Ossian Brohmer on the set of The Warehouse last Monday with up-and-coming actress Sabine Upsell.* I'm at the desk, in the role of Julia, looking up at Ossian as he gives some last-minute directions, waving his script in the air.

Louis flicks his laptop shut and lays it on the small wrought-iron table. He stands up and rests his hands on the balcony railings. "It seems quite busy down there today. Nothing like a bit of drama to get the hoi polloi scurrying around like headless chickens. I can see at least two vultures sniffing about with their zoom lenses… Look, you can see them from here!" Louis swivels round. "Hey, are you okay? Maybe you need to lie back down? What's up?"

I lick my dry lips; my heart feels tight and my throat hurts. My voice crumbles into a waver. "I'm just still in shock that someone I held in such high esteem for so many years, who I felt I loved, in a funny sort of way, expressed such anger and hatred… he seemed to *hate* me; he wanted me to *die*… I felt like my life had turned a corner…" I find myself sobbing helplessly, but continue, "…that there was some kind of God up there, making sure that I met the Director of *The Index of Dreams* after all these years; making sure that I had a reversal of fortune. That's what's supposed to happen in a film isn't it? Or at some point in your life, you think *finally….* you think… *now it all makes sense, this is what it was all leading to…* and, on top of everything else, I feel responsible."

"Hey! What the hell do you mean?"

I breathe in sea air in the warmth of September sun. I lick my lips again, tasting salt – from the air, or tears, or both.

"Because he was walking around this time last week like a normal person. He seemed *normal*. Okay, not *normal* – because Ossian Brohmer was too interesting to be normal. But he was walking around. He swam in the sea. We went on location. And then he flipped. It just seems a bit of a coincidence… why does he flip and kill himself just after meeting me?"

"Hey… Whoa! Whoa! You think it's because of *you*? You're taking the *blame*? Hang on a minute. This guy kidnaps you, basically, falsely imprisons you, tries to intimidate you into a suicide pact, drugs you… then realises he'd better kill himself as the police are going to be closing in… and you think it's *your fault*?"

"It just seems a bit of a coincidence… I wanted to

help him, but all I did was bring out his bad side… even the newspaper report makes me sound like a suspect… *'A thirty-five-year-old woman is helping police with their enquiries.'* Don't you think that sounds dodgy?"

"Whoa! Maybe you need to go in, go back to sleep for a while. You're exhausted, Beanie; you're getting paranoid."

"Can we just stay in the sun a bit longer. I need to warm up. It was freezing up at the police station."

"The good thing, Beanie, the good thing is that you can tell the world the truth, *the truth* about Ossian Brohmer. The truth about what happened. You could make some money out of it. Give an exclusive to *The Daily Fail* or something… By the way, did you know, the police even asked Rupe for a statement? So, now it's on police record, our first night of how we got it on, it will all be typed onto some police computer, to be encrypted probably at some point, recorded for posterity."

"Sorry about that."

"Don't be sorry. People love the drama of it all. Even Rupe."

"Doesn't it make you feel strange to think of Ossian Brohmer lying in a mortuary somewhere, his body cold. Maybe if I'd kept out of the way… not tried to make my life more exciting…"

"Beanie, let's just get one thing straight. It's not all about *you*. Ossian Brohmer had 55 years to create his life, make choices and sort himself out before he met you. Because you spent, what, thirty hours of your life hanging out with him last week, doesn't make you responsible for the fact that he'd got a drug problem, that he'd run out of money, that the police were already after him… Have we got that straight?"

"Mmm… okay, you're right. It just seems sad. If he'd just seen everything differently. We could have gone to the party last night. Gone on to make the film."

"He was too far gone, Beanie, … a victim of his own philosophy… committed suicide."

"But that's what was so sad. He didn't make a choice. It's like he'd gone into a tunnel and only seen a dead end. It wasn't like *The Index of Dreams* at all."

"You sound like you're saying you still *like* the film!"

"I do! It's just that after all those years spent in a funk… it's like I'd been a corpse, down at the bottom of a river, or a lake, weighed down by things; but then, a few millennia later, the weights dissolve, and you rise to the surface, the way a body floats to the surface… "

"Charming! Have you got any more good chat-up lines?"

Louis squints down at the street.

"Christ! I swear that photographer is pointing his zoom lens up here. Let's go inside…"

Dear Simon

I'm really looking forward to seeing you, too.

Yes, it's true that I'm 'the woman who escaped from Ossian's house' and yes, I did feel that I came quite close to death.

*I was never in a relationship with Ossian – other than…
how can I explain? Perhaps there was a part of me that didn't
feel safe in the world many years ago, and it's as though a part
of my soul departed and lived within The Index of Dreams in
order to survive. Sometimes when we feel under threat it feels
safer not to try and counter the threat, but to absorb it, and to
hide your real self somewhere else. And that's why I didn't
know where I was for many years, other than in the idea of
The Index of Dreams. But even then it's as though this idea
got found out and hunted down, censored; and then I felt
censored, too, invisible, without a voice.*

*So I just wanted to explain that, despite everything, I don't
hate Ossian Brohmer, or the memory of Ossian Brohmer,
although in the end he became a different kind of threat,
spinning a narcotic web of nightmares rather than
liberating ideas. He thought I'd jump at the chance to be in
a suicide pact with him, but the thing is… I think, at the
point he met me, I was like a prisoner who's been in prison
for many years who, despite the wasteland of their past and
their lost years, goes through this gate into the outer world
and thinks, "I'm still alive. Things haven't gone too well
and I don't have any great expectations left. But since I'm
still alive after all this time, I think I'll take a look around,
see what's out there, sit in the sun for a while. Small things."
And that's why I didn't want to die, even though I had
the chance.*

*I just wanted to explain all these things because I wanted to
tell you the truth about myself and I don't know how 'normal'
I am or how normal I can be. It's not true that I'm an
up-and-coming actress. I've never really managed to come*

close to being that much of an Alpha female. (Although someone did once describe me as an 'alfalfa female').

I'm not sure whether the best thing is for me just to live somewhere really quiet for a while and try to discover who I am outside of The Index of Dreams. This person who stepped out of a dream, a film, a box of cotton wool. That's why I don't hate Ossian, even though in the end he was terrifying. I guess I felt safe in his little dreamy cloud all those years when other things in the world meant I didn't feel very safe.

But, yes, you will be back in time for the next Chambre Magique. We could go together? Or maybe talk somewhere quiet?

Lots of love

from

Beanie xx

Acknowledgements

I am indebted to:

Zelly Restorick for the productive – and fun – brainstorming sessions, as well as her edits.

Jean-Philippe Touzeau for inspiring me to write this book.

Sophia McDougall at Cornerstones, Phil Nash and William Thomas for their invaluable feedback and suggestions.

Kim Lapworth and Sharon Gardner for their moral support.

Lorna Howarth and Rob Swan at The Write Factor for their expertise and help in the self-publication process.

Made in the USA
Charleston, SC
31 July 2016